THE MARTIANS OF OAKLAND

ANGELONER

authorHOUSE®

AuthorHouse™
1663 Liberty Drive
Bloomington, IN 47403
www.authorhouse.com
Phone: 1 (800) 839-8640

Published by AuthorHouse 02/18/2016

ISBN: 978-1-5049-6579-8 (sc)
ISBN: 978-1-5049-6578-1 (e)

Print information available on the last page.

Hi, my name is AngeLoner, and I feel that this story should be told. All I can really say is that this is the way that it happened in my life. I never entered the other world, the other world entered mine. As you read this story, you must know now I will say some thing's that may seem impossible to you, and as impossible as it may seem it really did actually happen, and it happened all around me and happened to me, and I lived it. For year's I was going to add fictional parts, but now I have figured out why I never published it that way, because I will just tell the truth, what took place, what I experienced, what I saw, and not only saw, but the clue's of what these living Alien's from another planet left behind, what I heard, smelled, witnessed and lived. Yes these Alien's from another planet are for real, and what I experienced, saw with my own two eye's and even smelled also the very evidence of their existence, the physical proof of these "things" and how some of them had lived in a Datsun hatchback car I had owned. I believe these Alien's was from the planet Mar's, because of photo's I had seen of rock sample's that fell to earth from Mar's. In the photo's show tiny sort of half moon shaped 'thing's', well as soon as I saw that I said to myself "those are 'Skeezer's', that's what I called them 'Skeezer's'. Except the one's in the rock were embedded and not to be known to move. But the one's I saw were moving, the one's I found were unbelievable, they were in the zillion's all stuck together on a oval shaped matter. They were all moving side to side all at one time's, a soft tone humming sound coming from them. At that time people didn't carry around cell phone's with camera's and video, I only had a pager. I thought perhap's it was some kind of a bug nest, but no, it wasn't, I know now it was those "Skeezer's" just like in the photo of the rock from the planet Mar's.

I'm telling this story mostly for people out there in this world, this planet Earth, to know of experience's that I have been through and have seen for myself about some of the evil's in the world also some of the good in this world, as I believe that there is more good than evil. Yet, I just don't know until this day why I've been permitted to see some of the thing's that I have seen, experience some unbelievable time's, all I know is that I have experienced it, and also seen it on the faces of many other people, after they have seen what I have, alot of which is unbelievable. The difference with this is I have physical evidence, I have seen physical evidence of these experiences, and in some cases smelled the odor's of these incredible experiences. Read on and keep your imagination open to this true story. Read of creature's from other dimension's, from Mar's, and the unexplainable yet proof based story's, and why I believe the "tiny creature's" were from Mar's. Also I write of other life changing experiences, that is good to read about because it can forewarn you, of what is out there.

This story goes back to some of my childhood, and move's around from chapter to chapter leaving it up to you to put it all together. I can't guarantee you that you will figure everything out before finishing this book, after all there are many mysteries in this world. How I've lived at the time and flashback's to year's earlier throughout my life. It is up to you the reader to decide for yourself which part's of my story are true or fantasy, my conclusion it's true. I call this story a "G" science fiction story, a new title of science fiction that I thought up, I've never heard ot "G" Science Fiction before this day, so when you do hear it again remember I am the person whom first came up with this title, with the emphasis on the G, which leave's the question that remain's, did this all happen, or didn't it? Which ever way, enjoy the reading, and I can say is yes this is the way it happened and it happened this way..............

CHAPTER ONE

The Black Room

I didn't have far to walk, since I had slept in the black room down the hallway there in the police station basement where I'm employed. Using my issued key's I unlocked the door to the custodian's locker room. I had slept that night at the police station, in the 'black room', I called it the 'black room' because it was pitch black in the room it had no window's, with only bunk bed's and later came one plugged in desk clock that lit up a small area of the pitch dark room, and a plug-in telephone. I secretly sleep in the 'black room many night's alone because the room I rent, on the top floor of a big 'ol mansion has turned to a scary nightmare to me, and I don't feel at ease or even safe living in the 'ol mansion. I had paid for the first and last month of rent and even a deposit, the guy I rented it from is only the manager, and not the owner he is also a rip off, as I found out. Sometime's I wonder to myself why was I doing Custodial work when I have a College Diploma for Medical Secretary. The answer must be truly just to have experienced what I have and write about it.

I was way early for work today, the first custodian there for the day, like many other days. I unlocked my locker and got my toothbrush, toothpaste, curling iron and my other personal and hygiene necessities that I would need to look presentable on the job for the day. I mean there was one day that I had gotten my purse ripped off by some thug's at the Bart train station on my way to work about five o'clock in the morning, and so my hair wasn't combed as neatly that day as it usually is, later that day a couple of the detective's noticed it right away, and mentioned it to one of the other custodian's that told me what they mentioned to him about why is my hair messy that day at work. I found the detective's to be very nosy. Why, the detective's had picked my back pocket with my wallet in it one day, yes they did.

But as far as my purse went the thug's at the Bart station had stolen my purse one morning on my way to work, that had my brush in my purse, thus why I hadn't brushed my hair that day when I got to work. As when I did sleep at my rented room in the 'Ol mansion I rode my bike to work in the cold early morning at 5:00 a.m., but they didn't steal my key's because I had my wallet in my pocket of my green city issued uniform pant's with a few dollar's. But the make-up I had just purchased, my hair brush and other item's were in my purse that day when it got stolen from the Bart train station.

But as far as the Detective's go, well they are just plain nosy. So from that day after I had my small purse ripped off at the Bart I keep extra supply's in my work locker that I may need at work. So those thug's had gotten my make-up that I had just bought, and other thing's that lady's use, but worst of all my I.D.'s and bill's of twenty's and even a picture of my kid's. I'm alway's aware of pick pocket's, but I didn't think that the young thug's would just run by me and snatch my purse right out of my hand the way that they did, and get away with it too! Damn bastard's! But then it is a everyday thing in the world around me, I didn't even bother to yell out for help or report it to the police. Heck what would they do anyway, they would never catch them, it would just be a waste of my time to report it.

Since I ride my bicycle to work, the day my hair style got all messed up from riding the bike and the wind blowing, I even asked my co-worker's if they had a comb or brush I could borrow, or even a hat to cover my messed up hair, but no one loaned me nothing to tidy myself up, and that's when the detective's on the second floor noticed the way I looked that day, that my hair wasn't styled for the day, as if it was my own fault or something, I couldn't help it if I had gotten my purse ripped off, but they were quick to judge me. Then it was another day the detective's picked my pocket for my wallet, like I said they were just being nosy. So they mentioned it to Hajit, one of my co-worker's, about my hair style being messy, although I alway;s dress neat and clean my hair was a mess that day. My title at the police station working as a civil servant is 'custodian,' cleaning office's, restroom's, mopping floor's and all the janitorial work that we do.

In the black room many a time as I lay there on the bunk bed thinking, it's the only place that I feel safe to sleep in now at this time, a safe place to live had become impossible for me. Since I had thrown out my x boyfriend from the tiny duplex we rented, he was a darn crack attic and I got tired of his addiction and him living with me going on about five year's. One day I just threw all his belongings into the drive way, he finially moved out by the time I got back that day. However he did pay half the rent for many year's but towards the end he stopped paying half the rent and started stealing money from my wallet. Oh, he was real slick about it because he would steal about half the money I would have in my wallet so that when I would go into my wallet there would be money there then usually one would automatically think there was no money stolen because there would be money there and would think that if someone stold money they would steal it all, so it took some time for me to realize that he was stealing money from my wallet, I guess it would be for his crack habit. I finially realized it one day when I woke up in the morning and I couldn't find my wallet, I was on my way to work and I told him I couldn't find my wallet and if he find's it he better not steal any of my money because i had the rent money in there. Well, that day when I got home from work, there just happened to be my wallet in the night stand next to my side of the bed. When I looked through my wallet there wasn't even enough money in there to pay the rent, so his game was over, I made sure he never stold from me again, because I slept with my wallet in my back pocket and I slept with my levi's on. Everything got worst at that point when he could no longer steal money from me, and the real nightmare got worst in the game's and trick's he played on me. I even got him a descent job which he is still working at to this day, he actually kept up with working there. Because of personal reason's I don't want to say where I got the job for him at, or his name. It bought some peace into my life breaking up with him. When he used to smoke his crack he acted so weird, sometime's like a 'fly' and other time's just weird. I couldn't take it anymore. Now of course I'm not perfect and I would drink my share of alcohol and smoke some weed, but I also kept up going to work and working for the City of Oakland, and I also have had other job's. I just would never stay anywhere too long, that was my problem, that I alway's kept moving on.

So I don't rake in alot of money for me to make much of a living on it's honest money and enough to get by on. It's all legal hard earned money, plus I don't depend on anyone else to find out where tomorrow's living will take me to. Only I just can't afford to pay alot for monthly rent here in the Oakland area, but I've alway's had enough money left to party with, and I would buy the alcohol for the poor 'so called' friend's that I let hang out with me, because they were alway's broke and never, ever shared anything with me. Yea, I learned to 'watch my back' because I know they would also steal from me. I soon became a loner mostly and liked it that way because at that time I had no true friend's. I have no one that I can rely on, just myself!

The people I hang out with, well they have their own live's. Every time I think that I can trust someone, they end up ripping me off, whether I know them or not. I know I'm being stalked, but who, exactly who are those people? I don't exactly know, but I mean to find out. There are just too many sign's of their existance, it is not just my imagination.

It has become a big problem to me, just at having a safe place to live without strange people or some creature's creeping around me, and being around me as I sleep alone, I've lived alone for a number of year's. My best friend's are my pet's, Loco which I will tell you about and my bare-eyed cockatoo Snoops, I've had her for many year's, and have kept her with me as I've moved from place to place. Sometime's I had to rent her a cage at a near by pet shop to keep Snoops at, while I move from place to place, trying to find a safe place for myself. And I don't just move from place to place with a piece of luggage. No, when I first lived alone everytime I would rent a room out of someone's home I had a moving company move me. I would move into a empty room and have the mover's carry in my own bedroom set, mattress and boxes filled with some of my belonging's, and a closet full of clothes. So I keep a small storage in San Leandro for my bigger item's I own, a storage that I thought my property would be safe at and untouched by thieve's, but they managed to get into my storage and rip-off alot of my good possession's I have stored there. I know this because I take inventory every now and then, and I am talking about a big storage company with my own storage room space. One of the maintenance people there that work's for the storage company told me before that the very on site manager's are responsible for stealing from people and that there is two different manager's that have the key's to it, but they get together and turn off the alarm system at night, then they use a master key that they keep hundred's of different key's and they open up storage's and go through people's property, and steal what they think no one will notice, in is by Marina & San Leandro Blvd. A customer won't usually find out until they move their belonging's out and go through their property then they will know that possession's are missing, but by then it is too late to do anything about it, unless they had insurance for their belonging's, which I never have. I have even seen an employee that had a big ring of dozen's of different key's on it. A place for safe keeping, bull shit, liar's. Damn thieve's, I hate thieve's!

I should have just rented places where there was furniture at already, instead of dragging furniture from place to place that I rented to live at. I just thought I would have been able to live at each place everytime for at least a year, but no the stalker's had me on the move. But at first for some reason it just didn't dawn on me to move around to furnished places, since none of the places I rented turned out to be a safe place to live. Beside's I had to have somewhere to store my personal property, picture's and whatever I have saved, kept and loved throughout my life. Too bad I didn't find out or even realize that the storage place ripped me off until later. But still, it sure is the pitt's that I have paid them thousand's of dollar's to keep my property safe, even with their alarm system yet they steal from me, and that mean's they steal from many other people too, and they get away with it. But now that I do know, and I wasn't insured, I can't do a thing about it. As a matter of fact I believe they had even purposely made me forget about one of my storage spaces, and kept that property of mine too, I mean an entire storage, and possibly could have auctioned it off, of course after they picked through it. I had about six different large storage space's at one time. So I would advise anyone that put's their possession's in a storage space to have it insured! When you watch these storage bid program's on television. I am sure that most of those spaces have allready been gone through and the best thing's have been all ready stolen and removed. But then of course they have to leave some thing's behind. I just know crooked people do those sort of thing's, I just like to think, and truly do believe that there is more good in this world than bad.

Please keep in mind that I have been writing this book since 1993, and here it is 2015. In 2002 we came to find out that my mother took sick, she got cancer of the lung's, yet never smoked a day in her life. My Mom had only told me and my Dad that she was sick, and she wanted it to stay that way. My husband and I moved in with my parent's so I could care for my mother helping with the cooking, and making sure my parent's made all of their doctor appointment's, took their medication's on time, prepared their meal's with food's they can eat and avoiding the food's they can't eat, and any other business task's they had to handle, or take them wherever they wanted to go. All throughout my life they would alway's direct me in the right path's to take in life, and forever giving me good advice. There was nothing they never had an answer for that they couldn't help me with. If I had any question in life I could speak to them, whether together or seperately, and there wasn't anything I wouldn't do for them.

But going back to 1993, My parent's at that time lived in San Leandro, California, I alway's would go and visit my parent's, usually everyday, but I don't bother them with my personel problem's., or at least try not to. And I've alway's been a person to keep personel thing's and matter's to myself, I hate complaining. I am the youngest child of six. My oldest three half brother's are from my mom's first marriage. When my oldest brother was very young in Hawaii my Mom took the bus with all the kid's to see new born kitten's at Grandma's house. My brother, so excited to see the kitten's ran out in front of the bus after getting off the bus and got ran over and died, God rest his soul. I've visited his grave in Hawaii, sure would love to have got to know my brother. My sister had moved to Las Vegas, Nevada and brother lives in Milpitas, California. Before moving in, all my life of adulthood I've lived close to my parent's, I visited them almost everyday, more than any of the other sibling's, and went shopping with my mom alot. We go to the Mall, Park, Flea Market's, Thrift Stores and visit family. Toward the end, Mom would take daily walk's with me through the park. I miss her alot, but I am so blessed to now care for my Dad whom is now 93 year's of age. It will be so wonderful if Dad make's a hundred year's old or more, we just found out that the President of the United State's mail's people that make a hundred year's of age a congragulation's, birthday wish, how wonderful.

My Grandparent's on my mother's side migrated to Hawaii on a steamship from Portugal. My Grandfather on my Dad's side was born in Bagio, Philippine's, and Grandmother in Hawaii. My Great Grandfather on my Dad's side was born in Corsica in the 1800's.

LOCO

Going back to the 1990's, there was only myself and my pet cockatoo, Snoops that lived in the huge home by Lake Merrit in Oakland, California. For week's I had lived there alone, and considered Snoop's my best friend. I enjoyed day's simply riding my bike, visiting my parent's home in San Leandro and buying a 6-pack of beer taking it to the Oakland shoreline, sipping up, playing my oldie music on the raidio and gazing out to the water, wondering where Loco was at. Ah yes, Loco, I can't forget Loco. Okay possibly out of all this story, Loco could have been my imagination, but then maybe not, because I just had no physical proof that there was ever a Loco. Let me share with you about Loco. Gosh, Wow, where do I begin with Loco. I guess how this started was one day as I gazed out to the Bay I saw what looked like a sort of scaled dark long snakish huge water snake sort of rise above the waters so I could see the top of his scales slither by in the water. After that day I would go by the water nearly everyday and do sort of a hummmm meditation to perhap's call him to me. I lived alone and stayed at some of the hardest part's of Oakland, and figured at night to meditate, hummmm to call Loco to me. Somehow I figured out Loco liked to eat cat's, as there became cat's in the neighborhood missing. Till one night after I meditated and hummed for Loco I looked outside into the street light lit yard, and I saw it a shadow of what I Loco would look like if he had risen above the water. It was a big shadow of a very good sized scaly backed snake looking animal with mouth open and fangy teeth. Mind you it was a shadow only that had soon disappeared into the night. So I am being honest about this, I just don't know if this one was real, however I got to find out that Loco only travelled at night on land and he moved very fast. Let's leave this at that.

Getting back to my Bare-Eyed Cockatoo, Snoops, when I first got Snoops I thought was a male but when she layed egg's at the bottom of her big cage I knew then she's a female. Snoops has been with me nearly 30 year's now. She's a beautiful bird and can sense when a stranger is around by screaching out to let me know. At once time though I moved around alot and paid for Snoop's to stay at a pet shop in San Leandro

I was so alone, and lived alone for three year's, just me and Snoops but Snoops brought me joy just by hanging out with me in the big drafty old home by Lake Merrit in Oakland, California. But I would have enjoyed the freedon and have enjoyed so many day's with a couple of bottle's of wine or a 12-pack of beer just sitting on the shoreline, enjoying the view, the waves and boat's passing by, with the wonderful different species of bird's, playing in the deep water's of the Bay. I loved to think of Loco out there in the deep water's, just swimming around to his heart's desire and having all the space that he need's. The whale's are so beautiful as they play in the deep water's, knowing I just need to hum and meditate to bring Loco closer.

So as time went by I had to find a job and that's when I got the custodian job at the police station in Oakland, I grew up in Oakland, the Bay area. After my kid's were grown and on their own, the way I moved from place to place I should have never had mover's move my furniture for me into the different places, I should have just travelled lightly, anyway I learned by now. Most of the places I've rented had gotten so spooky that I would sleep with all my clothes and my shoe's on. I even got Snoop's out of the pet shop to stay with me in the weird places, so that she could watch my back as I slept. Because as I slept if anything came close to me, Snoop's would let me know by screeching loudly, but I hadn't known about having Snoop's with me in the beginning of living alone, as you will soon read.

Working at my civil service job at about fourty hour's a week, I live off of that money, it's all good. I had no bill's except the cost of living, and no real bad habit's. Sure I drank sometime's, I expecially enjoyed drinking beer, and steered away from the hard stuff, like whiskey or tequilla. I also loved smoking marijuanna, but in the 1990's the weed just wasn't that strong, like it is nowadays, and it used to make one laugh alot, not now.

Some of the place's that I want to call home that I've rented in the East Bay Area have become unbearable to live at, I've never been able to call the different places home. It alway's happen's the same way, I looked for a room to rent in the newspaper's, or local paper's. I have no one that I know of that would rent a place of our own together, and none of my family would keep me for any longer than a couple of day's, only because they knew I could handle having a place to live alone, and I didn't want to burden my parent's with it, never letting on to them the danger's I face all the time.

Of course I would like to be closer to Loco there where he almost forever is, by the ocean, but now he has to come way inland to see me through water channel's, river's and lake's, as I explained earlier about Loco, truth or fantasy, this one I was never really sure of. I am so hesitant to tell my entire story, but then most of what I remember I will write, that I have decided on.

I had to find a descent place to live at with the little money that I made, I sure ain't about to get into no hoeing, stealing or anything shady like that, it just isn't my thing. Beside's I've known enough people that do those sort of thing's. But they would be people that hoped to be my friend and only to use me or steal from me, a passing thing, because for me, a true friend is hard to find. To have moral's and ethic's in the middle of all of this madness of partying, getting high, and trying to be a good person, is something not easy to accomplish! But I know I have something to accomplish for the United State's government.

Have you ever heard of the men in black, I guess the government has used me as a sort of 'woman in black'. Okay here goes, I had never meant to discover the 'Martians' from Mar's, my story here will explain. You've got to read this to understand that this is not just a possibility but a real fact and this did happen, as I saw with my own two eye's the Martians, they lived in my Datsun car at that time. Oh my gosh, when I think of it, it's something people must know had happened in my life. Even though I am taking the risk of people calling me crazy, well yea I can understand this, because I have watched shows on TV where people talk of there encounters with UFO's and Aliens, and some of those stories well I can't believe myself. Ah, but there is not one, no not one story that I have heard of where the Aliens actually lived with a person or people and made friend's with them. Just about every story I have ever heard of end's up being a nightmare and the Aliens had been mean to people or experimented on them or something awful.

I didn't want to live alone but I felt much better being alone than to be with someone that I can't trust, and each place I lived alone at, place after place since selling my home in Hayward, California and moving out, the rental place's became living nightmare's. It was some kind of an invisible force that followed me around, some good, and some bad. Places became science fiction mishap's, I just wouldn't know of any other way to explain it. I should have just moved around with a couple of suit cases, but instead I would hire a moving van to move boxes of clothes and my own bedroom furniture to each room I rented. Now I must admit that was dumb, I believe that deep down inside I wanted to build my own little world and my own small space and comfortable bedroom. But it just never worked out that way. People would con me into putting down the first and the last month rent, and a security deposit, then each place someone would go into my room when I was home, while I slept and sneek around to find what they could steal real quick from me, or even do other thing's. Even when I changed those lock's on my door somehow a place I rented managed to get the key to it, or pick the lock, there was just no keeping those bastard's or bitches out.

So for recreation I used to drink alot of beer, and smoke marijuanna, but I didn't over do it, I partyied for about twenty year's straight, starting in my twenty's. But one thing I hated was cocaine, still do, that I stayed away from, and I hate crack. I lived through a horrid life from 1988 to 1993 with a crack attick, so that's also why I hate cocaine and crack. I never did LSD or heroin either, too scary for me to try, no thanks. Okay I know what you must be thinking, "She was drinking and smoking marijuanna so she must have dreamed this all up. I say "NO" what I am saying is real and not fake, how I know this is because the Alien's left thing's behind, like their 'droppings' well you know their waste, their 'crap', it looked like long cigarette ashes, that a actual ciggaretter could not make as it stuck together rather well. Beside's I wasn't partying 24-7, I would eat pretty healthy, alway's love salad's, vegetable's and enjoyed my steak's. When I drank soda it would be sugar-free soda, probably what had saved me from ever getting sugar diabetes. Being 5'2", I weighed 130, with a nice waistline, me riding my bicycle to go everywhere, to work, to the store, to my storage, for recreation kept my weight and cholestrol down very well.

For year's, I had slept for only about three hour's a week, that's a week. But yea that was in the 1980's. As I got older I learned to get plenty of rest. After about 1996 I quit the smoking cigarettes, then I quit the alcohol, and finially quit the marijuanna, I just got tired of it all, and walla, no withdrawals, just quit. Probably no problem with it because I never 'had a jones for it' all'. I could have done with it or without it. But I did like my beer alot, and loved the loud music I played and listened to it, and loved dancing, loved dancing. Why I would put on my high heeled shoe's and jump on to the top of a table and do a sexy dance for my boyfriend at the time. Yes, I will admit, I loved to party, but mostly alone or with a guy I was with at that time. I never cared for a crowd, alway's been a loner. On the day's of my hangover's I smoked no weed, no alcohol no cigarettes, no nothing, just ate real well, relaxed, watched TV and pampered myself. But don't let me get to ahead of myself here all that quitting absolutely everything was in the later 1990's. And no A.A., no program's, no withdrawals, I just quit one at a time with monthly interval's. Although I had a few DUI's back then and the Court made me go to AA classes, I went to a few then didn't go back, I just had someone else sign my card's. This type of life will do that to you, plus the partying, they fit in together. But at that time when I slept those short hour's is not the time that I first discoved the 'Martians', that was in the 1980's. I discovered the Martian's in the early 1990's. I am putting this true story out there, believe it or not.

I drank my share of beer, and I lived alone, one day I finially realized that after awhile when I would become so intoxicated or so high, I became too high and intoxicated sometime's, and not altogether from what I was doing, yes I realize that some kind of a concoction that make's me sleep was being snuck and put into my beer's. I'm being stalked and the stalker or stalker's have even become to know what store I'm going to and before I go into the store, like when I buy some beer, they would know the brand of beer I drink too. So I realized that I have to be sure as to not go to the same store's and place's daily, in other word's I started to be sure not to make it into a regular daily timed schedule. It even came to where I had to start checking out every twist on beer bottle top's in the store before I buy the bottled beer, to make sure that it is not tampered with. How I discovered this is that I went to the usual store that I go to and at the usual same time everyday. I purchased the usual same beer I drink, took the six-pack to the park with me as I sat on a bench, I watched the guy's play basketball in the park. I twisted open the first beer top without really noticing that the beer top had been tampered with, but then I thought 'no', that can't be, I just bought the six-pack in the store and it was in the six-pack box, so no one got to it, or did they? Then when I went to open the second beer, I noticed that the top twisted off in a weird way, and even though the glass beer bottle top's seal wasn't broken, it was tampered with, and all the other's in that six-pack too. I had gotten so high from the first beer that if I had drank all the beer's I would have became too high by then, and passed out. Then I began to realize that must of been happening to me for sometime now, without me knowing it, I mean somehow buying the tampered with beer's. So I went back to the same store the next day at the same time I didn't say anything to the man cashier about the six-pack of beer I had purchased the day before. I just grabbed the first six-pack of beer that was the first on display for sale in the corner store cooler. I paid for the beer then when I got outside of the store I looked at the beer bottle top's real good, and those had been tampered with also just like the beer the day before. Someone had twisted the top off without breaking the seal of the bottled beer and must have dropped something inside. I had to show the clerk, he didn't want to believe it, but told me to get another six-pack. I got canned beer instead, need I say there is a way to mess with those too. From then on before I buy beer especially, I had checked the opening's of them and it kept happening over and over again. So I made it a point to change to different beer brand's sometime's. Because whomever it is doing this to me, has a plan.

I know that plan, it is to know my everyday's doing's so they can set me up when I drink at home and get high alone. The stalker is lurking in the shadow's somewhere, all the time, following me. But there's a slight twist here, I am alway's aware, and I practice everyday my one 'karate hit'. That's all I would need give a person one hit, enough to protect myself. I would even hit a brick wall bare knuckled without breaking my arm, or bleeding. The brick wall I just did a few time's, mostly I would hit a wood wall. I knew my fist was a lethal weapon. That's some of the reason I can't sleep when I am alone. I had to watch my own back before I bought Snoop's my Cockatoo with me, allthough I discovered later that Snoop's would watch my back it is better I found out late than never. I had Snoop's at a small pet shop in San Leandro called "Paradise Alley" for awhile because I had nowhere else to keep Snoop's, until I finally got Snoops out of there. After I proved that there really is someone entering my room at night as I sleep in the different 'dive's' I have been renting lately. Here is how I knew there was someone entering my room at night. Okay I wiped down both my bedroom nightstand's real good and clean, made sure there were no cigarette ashes or anyhing on there, then I put a new fresh book of matches there and a ashtray with a couple of coin's set exactly even next to each other. There was also a chair right next to that nightstand, a alarm clock and a lamp. I took a photographic picture of the setting in my mind since back in the early ninety's we only used pager's, and so I knew exactly the way it should look the next morning, turned off my light's, as the night moonlight shown through the window it wasn't completely dark. I went to sleep I had to wake up early ar 5 a.m. the next morning as usual to go to work for the City and be there by 6 a.m. I need a safe night's rest, living alone with no one else to watch my back. So sometime's I sleep in the black room where I work at for the City of Oakland Police Station, and where I feel safe at.

The next morning my alarm goes off at 5 a.m., upon awakening first thing I notice is a match gone from the book of matches, nothing else is gone except a few ashes in the ash tray. And no, those ashes were from a cigarette, not the type from the 'Aliens' droppings. Bam, someone was there. Another weird thing I had noticed when I awakened in the mornings sometime's that on my skin would be three tiny dot's each point at a triangle, and I had noticed this on several different occasions. Damn, who's stalking me what do they want, do they have anything to do with the Aliens'. I didn't know, and that I never found out.

~"An honest day's work"~

Living by Lake Merrit, I was only about 10 minute's to commute to the main police station, I got there early, so I could get ready for work, no one was there yet. I unlocked the Custodian's locker room and went to the mirror in the ladie's rest room. I stood there rolling up my hair with my curling iron, getting ready for work and putting on my make-up, in the ladies employee's locker room. I could hear the gun fire hitting the other side of the wall as the police officer's practice at their target's in the gun range room, we were located in the basement. Taking a quick glance at my pocket watch, I put my make-up on fast, because I know that at any minute one of the other custodian's would be getting to work, some people depending on which co-worker will blab to the head supervisor anything they can about anybody that isn't inside their 'circle of friend's,' there was also alot of nepotism there.

I try keeping a low profile, and minding my own business. Myself, I figure if the supervisor hear's anything negative about anybody it won't be from me, because I don't talk behind anyone's back. I knew of alot of crap that would go on, but I just shut up and keep it to myself. I guess that's because I am part Portuguese, and usually Portuguese people will alway's 'tell it like it is, like it T-I-IS, that's what my Mama alway's advised me to do, and I held on to that. Strangely enough I found that people begins telling you alot of their private live's and problem's they have. I would listen to them, but that would be as far as it would go. So I tell a person the way I feel to that person's face, and not behind their back. Usually if one person know's something about what another person is doing on the job that they are not supposed to be doing, there has to alway's be at least one other person that know's the same thing about that person, so I just leave it up to the other person to 'report' on it, I keep it to myself, and that goes for any job I have ever had anywhere, and I have had alot of job's, good one's too. In other word's I am not a nosy person.

Well, of course unless what they do is a constant danger to anyone else on the job then I would have to report it, whether I wanted to or not, it would have to be done. And I said 'on the job' not 'on the streets'. I grew up in East Oakland and you learn at a early age, what you know is what 'you know' and that is as far as it goes, you tell no one. Around the job, I simply keep to myself, I know some people do thing's that they shouldn't be doing, but I just turn the other way, and keep my mouth shut, like countless number's of other's do. Petty thing's are minor anyway.

~"Early to work"~

Although I was at work earlier than any one else in our department, it didn't matter much because some of the other female Custodian's would often get there early to take a few minute's to curl their hair too. As a matter of fact that is where I got that habit of getting ready at work from a co-worker. I mean they can do it, but you can't, I don't care about what someone else does, but there are alot of people out there that get into other people's business when they should just mind their own! And also at alot of work places some people get away with doing alot of things they should not be doing that other people can't do and end up getting fired for doing or written up. Now that's not fair.

"Good morning, AngeLoner," one of my fellow co-worker's that arrive's a little early greet's me.

"Good morning, Sally, how you doing today?" and so forth with the good morning greeting's. The first thing she does was hit the toilet. Oh darn, a bunch of shiting and farting was going on now, as there are two toilet stall's in the restroom. I quickly combed my curl's, got my belonging's together and got out of that restroom, put my stuff into my locker, punched my time card in for the day and headed outside for some fresh air. It was summer time and I could allready feel the heat at five fourty five in the morning. I walked across the street to the taqueria for a cup of morning coffee and a tamale. That would fill me up until lunch time, I don't eat much anyway, and keep my weight down that way, plus all the dancing I do and riding my bike.

I had 15 minutes to get me a tamale and coffe and get back across the street to work, I jay walked back across the street, walked in and took the elevator down to the basement where some of the custodian's were starting to gather in front of the covered windowed office of the supervisor. The custodian main office window is completely covered off by alot of work related paper's, like rules and OSHA paper's or announcement's to employee's. I thought to myself that if I were supervisor I would take down all those paper's and put them somewhere more appropriate. That way one could see out of the window into the hallway and what employee's were doing, it would be more like a communication thing. However I found out later why those paper's obstructed the office window's.

As the Custodian's were looking on the posted form on the wall at their work area's for the following month, I walk over to the posted item's and check to see what part of the building's I would be cleaning for the next month. Some people get moved around alot, and other's don't, they are usually the employee's with year's of service or P.C.'s, Privileged Character's, remember the nepotism. But then of course like everywhere else they have their favorite's. Then just as I am sipping on my cup of coffee and about to have a seat to eat my tamale for my breakfast, Larry the supervisor walk's over to me and ask's, "AngeLoner, clip my gold chain on for me will you?"

I set down my hot cup of coffee and tamale and clipped on his gold chain, jokingly I ask Larry, "Ou, that's a nice chain, can I have it?"

He look's at me and tell's me; "What! You better hurry and drink your coffee and eat your tamale before we start work."

"Excuse me Larry, how am I gonna enjoy my tamale and coffee when you ask me to do thing's for you, ah helll-o." We both laugh together, although I don't think that it was so funny, I just laughed to keep the peace between worker and supervisor, but I don't kiss no ass. I finish my tamale and coffee then go to sit in the lady's lounge until the other Custodian's are there.

"Howa you AngeLoner, what job you got today?" A co-worker Hajit ask's me.

"I gotta clean the first floor, burgulary, homicide, juvenile department and 911 on the other floor's. What a drag, but you know it isn't as bad as during the week end when I have to clean about 250 toilet's a day here. I know it is that much because I have counted them a couple of time's while working. Some of the toilet's look clean like they haven't been used, but I throw some disinfectant into them anyway, to be sure they are clean and check each stall. I noticed whoever is supposed to clean those area's on the other day's of the week, don't do some of the clean up that they are supposed to do but leave it for me to clean on the week-end, I'm tired of that!"

Hajit look's at me and shake's his head and say's, "Thiz iz becuz u alawez do it foror hem, dontta do it, letta hem do it."

Hajit is from India and doesn't speak english too well, but is a nice guy from what I know of him by working with him.

"So you know that we are working together in the afternoon, right?"

He look's me up and down and say's, "Ah yessa mam I knowa thez."

I thought to myself about how he looked at me and sorta wondered what he had in mind for me. I knew that he wanted to ask me something, I just didn't know what it was.

"Hajit, I will meet you after lunch right here, so we can do the special project the stuporvisor got for us to do."

"Oh, ha ha ha ha! He laugh's out so loud. "I likey thez onea, stupavisor, ha ha ha!"

"Aeioght thon, I'll see ya later."

"Oh, yezza, ok, ci u lata, AngeLoner."

All morning long as I worked by myself, and even though there were people all around me, I kept thinking about how I had to go back to the place I'm renting, back to that spooky room at the top of the flight's of stairs past each floor of the small apartment room's. I hate that place I've rented, it get's so spooky there, especially at night time as I sleep alone in my bed. I don't have to sleep alone, and could easily chose from a number of men I know and sometime's hang out with them, or let them hang out with me, but I know what they will want in return, sex, and that's not happening, well at least not unless I was serious about a man. So for that matter I sleep alone, for now. Until the day come's that I have a special man and special lover.

With people entering my room usually when I have gone out somewhere, and even while I am in a deep sleep, as I be sure to lock the door and bought that new lock, it just doesn't seem to make much of a difference. Possession's, beer and clothes of mine in my room are alway's missing, being stolen and I noticed my clothes were even being used by someone, weird ass M.F.'s. damcreepy thieve's. I was getting so tired of it, and knew the day would come when I would catch someone at something. As you read on you will find out not 'who' but 'what' I caught hiding in one of the hotel room's I rented.

But living this kind of life, living in rented room's that I can afford to pay on my own, I just wanted a small neat and safe place to live, since it is only temporary anyway, but then what isn't, still if I could find a place to live that is nice I would stay there for awhile. But it just wasn't happening, every time I moved each place only got worst and more frightening to live at. I even started sleeping with all my clothes on at night, my shoe's, sock's, blue jean's, belt, blouse and black leather jacket. Living alone in some of the dive's I had to live in, because of the low monthly rent payment's was all I could really afford to live at, since I supported myself, and my job doesn't pay that much. So for now I have to settle for living this kind of a life, living in cheap small room's, thank goodness my kid's are over 18, well except one, the one that was kidnapped at birth. I will tell you of what happened about that baby boy later in my book.

I know that there was something special I had to do for the government, I just didn't know what it was, yet as I haven't told you yet of how I discovered the Aliens. Moving from place to place because the place's I rent would never work out. And even some of the room's I rented out had scandalous landlord's, manager's or owner's. I know of their game, renting out room's, asking for the first month rent, the last month rent and a fat deposit. Then they do something to scare a tenant away, and end up keeping the deposit and last month rent. And if a renter want's the money back then they would have to take the owner to court and pay some kind of money which doesn't guarantee on getting the money back that was paid out to them. Surprisely so, this happen's more often than one may think that it does. I guess basically a person need's reciept's and keep them too.

~"Being stalked"~

There' s someone stalking me, who is it, who are they? It needed it to stop, it needed to end! Only Snoop's to watch my back as I slept, but sometime's I sleep so heavily that maybe I won't hear Snoop's when he screeches to alert me of danger. Little did I know then that the beer's I keep in my refrigerator had been spiked with some kind of drug that put's me out, and that's why I slept so heavilly, so glad I realized about the spiked beer's. There's no one around that could care less about a bird screeching or even loud music, nobody cared. Unless when Burt the manager of the room I rented out in the dark mansion of room's, he was also my neighbor and stayed in the studio next to my room. He had his own bathroom, I however had to walk down the hallway toa community bathroom.

"AngeLoner, AngeLoner, are you listening"?" One of my co-worker's was trying to get my attention, but I was so occupied working and thinking about this evening.

"Yea, whuz up?" It was Mrs. Wong. "Da ya wanna walka to china towna and get somae goud won-ton soupie fa lunchia? It's gouda fooda!"

"Oh no Mrs. Wong, I am going to lunch with Hajit, unless you would like to come along to?"

"Ahh, no tanks yu, seea yu."

I went back to work and cleaned my way past the traffic department, and past the homicide offices, some county offices then past burgulary, then to the detective department, and that is where I would alway's get alot of conversation, especially when I work past Mr. Hood's desk and in that office. He would alway's have a smile on his face, and he told alot of jokes. A tall, dark and handsome man, and of course everytime a man would interest me, he would alway's be married, or couldn't ever be serious about me. I just about alway's have sex on my mind anyway, I can't help it, especially when I'm around sexy looking men, and there are alot of those at the Police department, but I kept too much respect for the officer's and could never ever get up the nerve to ask any out for a cup of coffee, as much as I wanted to when I didn't see a wedding band and know a man is single I just couldn't ask. Beside's why would a police officer even be interested in a City Custodian.

~"Getting my pocket picked"~

After working my way past Mr. Hoods desk, dumping his trash can into the one I used on wheel's, I worked on. Then I felt a slight touch to my wallet, which I kept tucked into my back pocket of my loose fitting levi's, so I felt my back pocket to be sure that my wallet was still in my pocket, and I felt it was still there. Only it was a bit suspicious to me, so I started to walk to the lady's restroom where I could take out my wallet and inspect it, only on the way I emptied more trash from the other desk's on that level that took me an extra ten minute's, then I sort of forgot about the wallet by then.

Then when I got to the five foot wide corridor, "Oops, excuse me!" A younger detective, but not a new employee, bumped right into me, almost even ramming into me.

"That's okay," I replied, as I felt him take out my wallet again and then slip another wallet back into my back pocket, then I realized that the detective, very fast, had taken out a decoy wallet from earlier when I was at Mr. Hood's desk and had my back turned, he was sneaking my wallet back into my back pocket. I just knew that's what happened. Mr. Hood's must have picked my pocket for my wallet when I worked past his desk earlier. I know that's what they did to me, and it was those two with maybe other's in on it. They must of thought that I'm really stupid and that I wouldn't know what they were up to.

The detective then walked into the large office where there are many employee's work desk's. I started thinking of what had just happened, and I thought it out. Hood's picked my pocket first back in his office, put a decoy wallet in, and after searching through my wallet the younger detective purposely walked into me to take out the decoy and put my wallet back into my back pocket, after they went through my wallet. I should have went straight to the restroom and checked my wallet the minute I had first felt it picked by Hood's desk. But I am such a hard worker when I work and really I didn't have time to fool around when I worked as I had alot of work for that day, and usually everyday I was assigned to alot of work. But I never complained, as I am not a person to complain. However I did notice that one of my co-workers, whom was a older woman maybe a year from retirement, well she hardly ever worked, she would walk from floor to floor selling raffle ticket's or some other item's most of the time, and I wouldn't hardly see her the other time's. I knew this, but I wasn't mad about it, I had grown up to respect my elder's, so as usual I just shut up about it. Beside's she was a nice person. Now getting back to the pocket picking, I should have just pulled out the decoy wallet when it was first replaced temporarily in my back pocket with my own, 'personal' wallet, then I would have busted 'them' on the spot for sure. Only what could I have said, 'Where's my wallet that you picked out of my pocket, it has my drug's in there?' No, even though it is wrong what they did, it would have been worst if they would have 'busted' me for it's content's. Actually which could never have 'stuck' because they were breaking the law themselves. So actually they couldn't have busted me because they were invading my privacy, and I guess that's why they didn't do anything about it.

I then made my way out to the public restroom's in the hallway, and went into a toilet stall, then took out my wallet from my back pocket and looked inside of it. When I looked inside of my wallet, sure enough, by the messed up way my wallet looked, with tiny bit's of marijuanna in my wallet scattered all over. Yes, I had a little weed in a tiny plastic bag tucked away in there, which I know that I shouldn't carry with me anywhere, let alone to work at a police station, but it was only for my personel use and if I left it at the 'ol mansion at that time with people sneaking into my room they would have smoked it up and probably replaced it with parsley or something, and who know's what that would be, because that is the way that thing's were happening around the place's I rented. It was for my own personal use, it was such a small amount, and I didn't smoke any earlier, and wouldn't smoke any until the evening. From that time on I kept my wallet deep in my front pocket when I went to work.

'Hmmmm, I thought to myself, I wonder how many time's before I had my pocket picked by them? And why was the tiny bag of weed opened, did he take a tiny bit of it to test, or did he take some to smoke himself? Just what was that detective up to, and why isn't he out there on his beat busting people for big time crime's anyway, why was he so damn concerned about me. I wasn't bothering anyone, beside's what ever made him be so nosy, and how many other people's pocket's were being picked beside's mine?

I am a single woman and I have no one to pay my bill's for me, this job I have here working for the city of Oakland is my only mean's of income, I live off of the money from this civil service job. So for my cost of living here and keeping up with my bill's doesn't leave me with much every month. But I make a honest living and alway's have.

I know alot of people, and even though I hang out with them sometime's, I am still a loner, and stay mostly to myself. Beside's I've never had a really close best friend that I could trust. Allthough I have a couple friend's that could be trusted but they live in another state, and a couple here, but I'm just not close to anyone. I'm also not the type to bother anyone, if they don't want me around then I'm gone. And that is exactly why I keep to myself, I had never met up with a trust worthy friend that I hung out with for year's, never in my entire life. Associate's and professional people don't count. Every friend I have ever had turned out to be a back stabber. Talk nice to your face and talk about you or try to rip you off behind your back. Anyway as this story goes on you will find out about my misson, or was it a mission, what about the Alien's from Mar's, was I the only one that wouldn't have freaked out when I found them in that restroom early that morning?

~"Quitting Marijuanna"~

'Okay,' I thought to myself, 'so I am wrong to carry marijuanna on me, but now the detective's knew and they didn't do anything about it'. Beside's it was such a tiny amount. I don't see how they would be able to legally do anything about it now anyway, since they picked my pocket. Beside's I am not a dealer, just a user, it was a tiny amount, and I had to deal with having to smoke the MJ anyway. Heck, what's the big deal, marijuanna nowadays is used for medicinal reason's, and that's the way it alway's should have been. Alcohol is way worst that MJ. But physically MJ is hard on the lung's. In my wallet, I made sure I had my phone numbers that were in my phone list changed and scrambled up so they would not be able to know who I would call from phone booth's. I don't steal from anyone, or don't do shady thing's, I pay for it with my hard working, tax paying job. It's not that expensive and only cost's a few buck's a week, that's how little amount of weed I smoke. I've never felt like I'm addicted, because I have it under control. I don't smoke crack, as I've alway's hated cocaine, especially that I had a x-boyfriend that lived with me whom was a crack addict, I'm so glad I got out of that relationship. I didn't do hard drug's, or drink on the job.

Now my mission, is a whole different thing, I am doing this mission why, I don't know but I do know that I will find out why, it sure is not for the money, what money I wasn't getting paid any money for this mission. By the way "what mission", no, not even the CIA can fool me on this one, HA! It will all come out in the wash sooner or later, at least to me I knew, I hope, even though I'm sure I will be the only one to know and now you will too. I do know that it is a good thing, and nearly an impossible mission, hey yea 'mission impossible', I will make it possible.

But why did the detective's find me so interesting, well I couldn't figure that one out, or were they just being nosy. After I came back to the floor where my pocket was picked at, Hood's approaches me and say's; "AngeLoner, you sure do look shakey to me." And I know what he was talking about because of the content's in my wallet, the drug's. But then that was my personel business anyway, and it wasn't right for them to pick my pocket and I guess that's why they never did a thing about the drug's in my pocket while I was at work at the police station. Because they know it is wrong to invade my privacy by picking my pocket.

I knew what he was talking about but actually neither of us could say nothing to the other, just like the mission. I was doing something wrong, but then so did they by picking my pocket, and invading my privacy.

So I told him; "I'm not shakey," and I held out my hand's in front of me, "Look at my hand's they are as steady as a rock."

Well Hood's never treated me the same after that, when I got to his desk he no longer joked with me the way he used to. And the other dectective's avoided me all together after that. The thing with that is, they are the one's that invaded my privacy by picking my pocket, hmmm I got the idea of picking one of their pocket's without them knowing it and see how that detective would feel. Anyway from then on I kept my wallet in my front pocket while I worked, to avoid from having my pocket picked, because I sure wasn't gonna leave my wallet in my locker, because I knew for sure the custodian's would go through my locker. I actually liked being a custodian thcrc at the police station, the undercover or the police throw away alot of good stuff that they take from people, some of the Custodian's take throw away stuff. But then there is alot of nasty stuff too, like rape victim's pantie's and other item's that is put into sealed up plastic bag's that are marked with an identity number, then after they are done presenting them for evidence or whatever, and they do their spring cleaning, well somebody has to throw all that stuff away and that would be the custodian's, I use glove's and of course toss that kind of stuff away to the garbage. But sometime's there is alot of neat stuff like digital scale's, nice wooden carved boxes, that people would have kept their stash in, that was now empty. I found a leather and suede back pack that I had given to my boyfriend at that time. I shouldn't have given it to him though, heck he never gave me anything except his messed up life and wasted time and for me to have let him live with me, was a total mistake. You will read about this now x-boyfriend, no names mentioned here, you'll read about him in chapter's ahead. Beside's whatever us Custodian's didn't take from the trash, we would empty outside into the big trash bin's and nobody, except me would ever bother to lock the gate's to keep the public from going through the trash and taking what they wanted. There had been many a time that I would shread important paper's, and I mean top secret paper's that would just be tossed into a bin, and would be thrown into a recycle bin that the public garbage picker's would have access to and take, because nobody bothered to lock the gate till the garbage men came to pick it up. But then I thought about it, even the garbage people could go through all those important paper's, heck I couldn't shread them all, I didn't work seven day's a week, and the other Custodian's just didn't give a damn about it. Also some Custodian's didn't even realize what important paper's were being tossed without being shreaded first. That's like a security breach, I told the supervisor Mr. Jones about it, but he didn't give a darn either, and just told me to simply empty it all into the recycle bin's.

One of the Custodian's told me that she had found $350.00 in cash, when she went through the trash from undercover agent's, but she didn't bother to turn it in and kept it. But I know myself, that if I would have found any money I would turn it in, because that is just the way I am. One day as I was cleaning the juvenile jail section, I found $19.00 on the floor and turned it in the officer that would sit at a desk in that office on the week-ends. But when it came to lunch time and I checked my pocket's for my own money, I realized that it was my own money that I found on the floor and turned in. I had accidently pulled it out of my pocket when I had pulled out a new plastic bag from my pocket to reline the trash can's. It was my job and I stayed true to it every minute on duty, well except for the sex thing and having sex on duty, that I couldn't resist, beside's we weren't hurting anyone by doing so on duty, I'll tell you later about that little episode. Only that happened at one of the recreation center's, with one of my supervisor's.

PICK POCKET'S

A person that pick's pocket's can do it so fast that most people wouldn't even notice what took place, but not me I'm too fast, I felt a Detective pick my pocket, I just didn't believe it enough to take out the decoy wallet that was planted into my pocket, by a Detective, while my wallet was being looked through, I just didn't kknow it at the time. Now I just alway's stay alert to everything around me, people, places, sound's, smell's, all that stuff. And that was something new to me, I mean about slipping a decoy wallet into my pocket, so when the person get's their pocket picked and feel's to see if their wallet is still there, they feel the decoy one and won't know that they got their pocket picked until later, or maybe not at all, if the pick pocket will be around to slip your wallet back and get the decoy wallet. If their smart enough later when they inspect their wallet to see if any of the content's are a different way from the way they had it, then be surprised at the finding's. Anyway, those detective's weren't slick enough to fool me, who know's what they were looking for anyway. Beside's the most important thing is my 'fathom' cover wasn't broken.

The police officer's and employee's working at the police station are so kind, such good people, of course, or this world would be in real bad shape if that weren't so. The experiences I've had working in the same building, as I met up with different employee's daily while doing my custodian job and keeping their offices clean, being in their office's they would usually be at work at their desk's. What a good way to get to know people, is at your job. Thank God for the good and honest police officer's out there in this world. But so sad for the bad one's.

I had my rent money rolled up in a rubber band in my front pocket of my baggy jean's, baggy jean's were fashionable then, I kept that money seperate, I had no checking or savings account, at least not that I knew of at that time. I didn't even pull it out of my pocket to see if it was still there or not, I could feel the rolled up money against my leg, the same way that I should have kept my wallet in my front pocket, not my back pocket.

Sooner than I knew it, it was lunch time, I met up with Hajit and we walked to the wharf at Jack London Square, only a few block's away from the station. I enjoyed watching the soft tide's flow in and out, and feeding the seagull's some of my lunch. If I held up some bread in my hand, a seagull would swoop down and get the bread right out of my hand, but I had to be sure that the bread was a big piece because I didn't want a seagull to accidently grab one of my finger's too.

"What foar lunchy, AngeLoner?"

"I told you dude, you speak good English for a person that has just been here a few year's, I mean I sure can't talk your language".

"Oh, thank, butta thana you donta cali me dude.'

"Ok, I understand, it's just a kind of fad word, it come's around for awhile then goes away and come's back decade's later".."

"Decades latar, whal, whazza deiel?"

"Oh, never mind, anyway what you talking about, what's for lunch, you asked me to lunch, beside's we just had lunch those two sandwiches, that's enough for me. And I did share one of my sandwiches with you. I shold be asking 'what's for lunch'. Hajit was a con man, and usually talked his way into me buying his lunch and mine, but not today. I think he sort of used his good look's to get his way with me, he knew I have a weakness for good looking men. He would alway's brag about how rich his father is, and even showed me a check made out to him, from his father in India, it was for $12,000.00. Only that didn't phase me one bit, not interested in just a rich man, I needed true love, and that sure wasn't gonna be me and Hajit, only friendship. But what get's me is, he brag's about all the money he has, and show's me the check, like I would give a dang, and what does that all mean, that mean's I pay for the lunch, and he is cheap. So his outer look's weren't so bad, but his inner self was greedy, but still a nice guy.

"Oh, AngeLoner, you ara a veddy prettie ladie, do u have a boyafriend?"

"No, I don't have a boyfriend that I'm serious about right now, I told you that a while back, how you forget so easily?"

"Angel, wha tha meen, sedious?" Hajit say's to me with his big smile of teeth.

"Serious mean's for real, that's what it mean's. No, I don't have a boyfriend now, ok."

"Wella, I likey u to met Harry, mya firiend."

"What, Harry, but I thought,........"

"Yea, I found youda namber agin thisa mornin, I just give to Harry today. Donta woddy, thets ok AngeLoner, he is a veddy gad gie!"

I turn to him, as we are eating our lunch, and trying to figure out what he is saying. "A gad gie? Whuz that, dude, oops sorry, oh you mean, Gad gie, gad gie, oh, good guy!"

"Yessa, yessa, gooood guy!"

"Well since you allready gave this Harry guy my number I will talk with him whenever he decide's to call me. But I don't usually do this sort of thing".

I kinda knew I would never be interested in Harry, but then maybe for a friend, just maybe I would be lucky enough to have Harry as a friend. Only men don't usually care to have women as their friend's, unless of course sex come's with it. Allthough nowaday's I see alot of celebrity women with gay men friend's, which are usually hired as an asistant than turn into a close friend. I don't see nothing wrong with that, one is lucky to have a true friend in this world. But then celebrity's usually have the fortune and fame and who wouldn't want to be their friend.

The work day went by so fast as usual, I kept myself busy. But after work I would have to go back to that damn heck hole that I live in. Even though I kept my rented room clean, it was a heck hole to me because people would sneak into my room while I either wasn't there or as I slept. Whoever they were would go through my property, even my personal belonging's, and just steal from me what ever they wanted to, or even go into my tiny refrigerator and drink my cold beer's that I would have put in there for me to drink a cold one when I got home from a hard day's work for the City. I just couldn't catch them at it, yet, that is. A lock on my door, to them meant nothing, just anothing thing to 'pick'. None of us are perfect, no not one, "For all have sinned and come short of the glory of God". For you see, I am a Born Again Christian. I was reborn when I was only 15 year's of age. But yes, throughout the year's I have back slid, but still stay with the word all I can. Sinning is not a practice to me, but those day's of smoking and drinking alcohol are gone. Throughout my life I would quit sometime's. I was first Baptized when Iwas 21 year's of age. But then year's later I went back to that sinning, allthough most of the time I kept reading the Holy Bible even when living that kind of life. It's not a sin to drink alcohol, it's a sin to be drunk. I have no opinion of marijuanna because it is used for medicinal reason's. Of course now here in 2016 I no longer drink alcohol, I haven't had a desire for alcohol since 2001, but last time I drank beer and got drunk was 2002 after my Mama passed away, that was it for me. I don't smoke MJ anymore because I can't it has bad affect's on me because of the cholestrol medication that I have to take, other word's I probably would smoke MJ.

What weird places I had chosen to live at, when I went to check out each place as I had to move from place to place, the places seemed okay at that time, but once I would move into a place, it would alway's become frightening places to dwell. Each place would be sure that they would get their money for rent for the first and last month, and even a security deposit, which is alway's bullshit because one never get's back a security deposit, hardly ever, even if they leave the place clean. How can people be that way, I mean what's a few hundred dollar's or more, which will probably soon be spent anyway compared to being honest. Since I wanted to have a place to live close to my job in Oakland, and couldn't afford to pay much with my part time civil service job, plus I had no benefit's, that's how places get over when they employ part timer's, that sometime's work full time, just give them no benefit's, it became a struggle for me. Only these places of residence were basically people that rent a room out just to get two month's rent and deposit, then they evade one's privacy until the renter begin's to hate living there, and soon are forced to move out, or even run out of there, and then the renter doesn't get back their money, only to find another cheap place and the same cycle happen's all over again. So then the people renting out a room will do the same thing to the next person, and that way they can make thousand's of tax free dollar's extra a year. It's just a game people play, I found that much out. The heck I was going through living in the dive's I had to live in and trying to stay safe with all the creep's that hung around that I didn't know, sometime's hung out outside my door, who are they? I didn't know, but some lived in the ol' mansion, I knew that much. I knew that whenever I put my drink down at the ol' mansion that I found out someone was sneaking into my room while I slept or even for a minute when I would go down the hall to use the community bathroom, I realized that people were sneaking into my room and even dropping something into my drink's that would soon make me sleepy and pass out. It didn't take too long for me to realize what they were up to for me to finially take my drink with me to the bathroom down the hallway and my key's and lock my door for those few minute's, that only slowed down their entry into my room and privacy. And that is all it would take is a minute for someone to sneak into my room and spike my drink or beer, so that is when it would happen, and I noticed it would be when I would drink and get real high it was alway's when I left my drink behind that when I came back to it I would get so groggy fast after sipping on the drink, and that someone was dropping something into my drink to make me that way. I would never get high that fast when I drank around people I know. But who and why? I could only guess at those reason's and the reason's I came up with were scary.

I would have to move from place to place so fast, and I would continue to do so until I found a safe place to live, and that is why I slept in the 'black room' often, because I could sleep well there, and feel safe there. I kept my belonging's in a storage space in San Leandro, it was a garage size, I've alway's owned alot, and I only had a few of my belonging's with me, but then I went and bought me that new bed and mattress, and took it to the ol' mansion, so the furniture I would use everytime would be my own furniture, oh if only I had thought of just renting room's that were allready furnished all the time, I would have saved alot of time and money, I just couldn't stand the thought of sleeping in someone else's bed. Even when I rented a motel room, I never get under the cover's, but laid my own blanket on top of the bed cover then covered myself with another one of my own blanket's, and my own pillow. But I had to keep some of my possession's in a storage closer to me, that took up more of my income too, because I owned alot of thing's. Like furniture, clothes, knick knacks, jewelry, wall picture's, just the regular house furnishing's, over a thousand doll's and action figure's. I have so many, Michael Jackson, Elizabeth Taylor, Elvis Presley, Sonny & Cher, John Belushi, Muhammad Ali, Frankenstein, Mummy, Werewolf, Munster's, almost all the original Puppet Master's, Sport Bobblehead's, Janis Joplin, Alice in Wonderland, Johnny Depp's different character's, Madonna, Britney Spear's, Anna Nicole, Vanilla Ice, Snoop Dog, Bruce Lee, Chucky, Star War's, Star Trek, Mickey & Minnie Mouse, Goofey, Pee Wee Herman, Daffy Duck, 007, Clark Gable, Beetlejuice, Winnie the Pooh, Puppet's, Hello Kitty, American Indian

Doll's, Pimp doll, Princess Diana, Kennedy Dolls, Jackie Kennedy, Shirley Temple, Marie Osmond doll's, Osbourn Family, Wrestler's., Campbell Soup, Kewpie doll's Bratz, Barbie's, James Dean, Twilight doll's, Fairy's, Beatle's, Patty Play Pal, sing and dancing Pinnochio, Little Red Riding Hood and old school character's, hundred's of elephant's made of ivory, LEGO's, wood, steel, rock, paper well you name it, I probably got it. And so many doll's.

I love to party and partying took up all my spare time, I just didn't feel like looking for another job, it would take up too much time. Although I have had many a good job in my time, a job twice with the County of Alameda, I worked two different positions for the City of Oakland, a job with the City of Berkeley. I delivered mail for the United States Post Office and also a Mailhandler for them. I worked for Hayward, Castro Valley and Union City Unified School Districts, then I have had a few other job's here and there. I had never been fired froma job, but I just would quit and move to another job. The thing with that is I should have stuck to at least one of those good job's for more than 10 year's straight so I could have collected more social security and their retirement benefit's package, seem's I never considered that, what a mistake. I have a high school diploma and a college diploma, but with all the competition, it would take up alot of time to look for a better job, but then maybe I would get fed up with all the bullshit, and just try to find a better job anyway. I couldn't live with any of my family they figured that I'm a strong woman and can make it out there on my own, so none of my family let me live with them for more than a couple of day's then they would tell me I would have to 'go home now'. If they only knew that I didn't feel safe at all, I mean with that damn stalker hanging around the places I lived, no matter where I moved to. Who was it, who were they, why did they sneak around me while I slept, drop thing's into my drink to make me sleepy, and what did they want? I was just gonna have to try to find out, some way or another I would have to find out. I just wanted to be left alone, but sooner or later, the damn stalker or stalker's would find me and start sneaking into my place whether I was gone or in a deep sleep, all I needed was a safe place to live, everyone thought that I could handle it myself, but little did they know what was happening all around me. Since the rent at the ol' mansion was paid up for another month and they had a deposit fee, I had the place to live in but got frightened there, and I hated it there because of the weird happening's there. It was just so strange, I noticed that when I woke up many morning's that I would find three tiny mark's on me, each mark like a tiny, tiny mark made a three point pattern at each mark at the point's like at point's of a pyramid. What is it? Never found out until strangely enough one day I saw on television on a station that had program's on Alien's and UFO's that some people would wake up in the morning with the same mark's I had.

The next morning, I had to work at a Recreation Center in Oakland, got there early and nobody was there yet, so I couldn't get in. My Dad gave me a ride to work that morning, he asked me if I wanted for him to wait with me for an employee whom had the keys to get in. I told him 'No', I would just sit on the bench outside and wait, so he pulled off in his car. About ten minutes later, I gazed away to across the big grassy field and I could see three, very big dog's. I thought to myself "Oh, heck, what am I gonna do now, because nobody else was around and there was just no where for me to go to get away from those very big dog's. So I started to walk around the building to the other side, then right there facing me head on were the big dog's. One Pitbull, one Rotweiller, and one bulldog. I knew I was in trouble then, but my year's of experience working at the Zoo with the elephant's and all those exotic animal's, well all that experience kicked in. I had no mace or anything to protect myself on me, so I just waved my hand to the dog's and told them, "Come on, let's go", kind of playfully. The three dog's ran with me for about twenty feet, then they began to circle me, bark and growl at me, good thing there was a garbage can container there that I grabbed on to and propped it in front of me, as I followed each dog's move. I thought quickly about how I would protect myself, so I acted like I had a toy or something in my hand, and just gestured to throw it and commanded to the dog's, "Go get it boy, go get it." While the three very mean dog's ran toward where I threw the imaginary object, I took off and ran to a high cyclone fence and climbed to the top of it. The three viscious dog's were beneath me on the ground circling around. Wow, I sure was lucky to have known what to do, if I didn't know what to do those three dog's would have attacked me, biten me and harm me. I waited at the top of the cyclone fence, hanging on up there while the three dog's finially ran back across the grassy field. Then when I knew it was safe to get back down from the fence, I climbed back down to the bottom and grabbed a big brick, then signaled to the three dog's afar off, and called them back. They ran back to me, but of course I climbed back up the fence. I was going to drop that big brick on top of one of those dog's head's. But I just couldn't do that, I love dog's, and all animal's, and just couldn't ever harm any. So again the three dog's ran off, and the employee with the key's to the Recreation center finially showed up. With the dog's gone by now, I climbed back down and me and the employee went inside the building. I told her what had happened and she told me that quite a few people were complining about those dog's being viscious and scaring people. I never told my supervisor what had happened and that the other employee was so late to work. Come to find out that other employee was the supervisors Niece. I also found out that she had told him she saw me sitting around in the basketball court area doing nothing. Which was a lie, because at that time when I was in the basketball court sitting down, I was on my break. I found out throughout the year's that there are some snitching, lieing employee's who tell the supervisors thing's people do and lie about thing's too. Like there was another employee at another spot that told the supervisor some lie about me, it was so stupid, I don't even remember what it was. Now that same employee used to take her laundry to the recreation center, a different one, a she used to do her laundry there, then fold all her clothes. She even used to style wig's while she was on duty. But I never went back and told our supervisor about that. The people whom tell suervisor's thing's and even lie's are usually the worst one's that do worst thing's. Can't stand those kind people who mind everyone's business, except there own business.

CHAPTER TWO

THE OL' MANSION

Yes, that ol' mansion was weird okay. But I watched out for what was going on all around me, and it only took a couple of week's after I had moved in to there that I knew I had to move out of there and I hated that damn mansion because of the intrusion's into my room while I lay down to sleep there, alone, or when I wasn't there, some asshole's would enter my room to see what they could steal, changing the lock didn't work, they still somehow got in. Why couldn't they just come out in the open and talk with me, what kind of weird shit was this that was going on, and why was it happening to me? It was a rude intruding into my personal life. One day I hoped to catch them and rid of the problem of whomever or whatever was going on. Like one night when I heard a window open and shut real fast. I turned to see what was going on, and could see a shadow outside of someonw jumping off the third floor roof that make a ledge just below the set of big window's in the rented room I stay in. Whoever it was, was gone so fast that I wasn't gonna jump out on to the roof

51

top to run after them or down the flight's of stair's
to catch them, as they would be gone by the time I
got to the bottom of the stair's and run around the
front of the house. After I locked that window that
was just slammed down from the outside roof top,
I happened to look down and saw that whoever it
was had just dropped a centipede on to the floor of
my room, and it was a huge centipede too, and fast
at creeping away. I just happened to have a big glass
cup near by and caught the centipede by putting the
glass over it before it got away. There's no way that
I had just imagined that, I saw the dark shadow of
someone jumping from roof to roof top right after
I heard the window slam down shut, and there was
that big ugly bug. After I caught the centipede in the
glass I got a magazine to push the bug into the glass,
opened the window back up and let the centipede go
outside of the window. I alway's made sure that my
window's were locked after that, after all I didn't
think that there would be anyone climbing up that
high to open my window. After that night the next
day I went to the hardware store and purchased
some wood puttly to seal up all the crack's that the
wind blew through, it took me two hour's to do
that. Only the next day when I got back from the
store someone had entered my room again when I
was gone and undid all the work I did on them darn
window's, and again the wind blew through. What
kind of weird people is this, why do they bother
trying to frighten me with all the crap they do?

Then a couple of day's later when I was about
to reach into some handwipe's that I had bought
from the drugstore a couple of day's before and I

had used a few handwipe's allready, but made sure I closed the plastic container real tight after each use, but this time when I went to get a handwipe to sanitize my hand's because i didn't want to walk down the hallway to the public restroom there in the ol' mansion, I just used the handwipe's to wash my hand's. Then as I went to grab a handwipe I noticed a small dark thing, I looked closer and it was a tiny centipede, there in the handwipe's. I knew for sure then that whoever was sneaking into my room, liked to play game's on me, and that it would backfire on them sooner or later. I threw away the entire container with the handwipe's inside, even though I had only used it a few time's, I wouldn't use anything with bug's inside of it. The 'ol mansion is for sure weird, what the heck is going on here. What really bothered me and scarde me is that at night time when I slept, someone would sneak into my room. I slept heavily in a deep sleep when I fell asleep, I know there is someone sneaking into my room while I sleep though. But who is this mysterious person, who is it what do they want from me. When ever I drink anything out of a can, before I go to the bathroom down the hallway I either finish the drink first or take it with me, and even lock my door. I figured it out by now that someone had a key to my room, because when I changed the lock and got back home just as I finished changing the lock I noticed that I just put on the same lock with the same key as the old one on, even though I had just bought the new lock from a hardware down the street that was a completely different key, and that happened when I went to the bathroom down the hallway for only a couple of minute's and left the door unlocked with the new lock there that I had just bought from the hardware store down the street. Someone had switched my new lock with the same old lock and key set. That was hard work changing the door lock, that was the last time I left my door open when I went to the bathroom down the hallway, from that time on I took my key's with me. I mean I am so straight laced in doing thing's. I guess it didn't make much sense locking the door for those few minute's, because someone had the key to my place. I'm such a considerate person that I didn't put on a combination lock because it wouldn't look right with a big latch from outside the door, but let me tell you if that were today, I would do that put a big latch outside the door with even a double lock, one key lock and one combination lock. I am still straight laced in doing thing's, only now I have more knowledge. But then again, the creep's probably would have figured another way to get into my room, like somehow through the ceiling, that darn hole in the ceiling that was there when I moved in, well actually it is more like a square hole, perhap's a trap door, oh I don't know, but it is there and open to the attic perhap's. Ah yes the attic where those weird noised come from, the noised of pidgeon's, and so that does tell me that there is a opening to the outside somewhere. You ever heard pidgeon's cooing? The cooing isn't so bad, but let me tell you other than the cooing they can make some pretty weird noise's.

I figured Alix the manager's ex that often sleep's at his place, well I figured she was the thief that switched my new key and lock back to the old key and lock because she was there when I was putting the new lock in. She hardly ever come's out of Burt's room, yet she did that time that I was changing the key and lock to the door. She asked me what I was doing, I told her that I was changing the key and lock because some asshole has been sneaking into my room, and dont' let me catch them! Alix had switched the round circle inside of the lock when I went to the bathroom, so that her and Burt would have the key to my place to steal from me, I know it was her. I just didn't feel like changing the lock again right away, I'm not a locksmith and that was hard to do. That damn biotch Alix sure is nosy, what fricking business is it of her's anyway. Heck, it must be her that was using my clean clothes out of my closet, I knew someone was actually suing my clean close one day, and then throwing them on my closet foor day's later, dirty. So when I went to the laundromat to wash my clothes, I stopped bringing all my nice clean clothes back to the 'ol mansion, I just took them to my storage. Also everytime Snoop's saw Alix she shreaked out so loud, she doesn't do that unless there is danger, and she was telling me that Alix was trouble and up to no good. Like one time when I had went to the local drugstore and bought alot of new makeup and lipstick and real good expensive mascara, I know what I bought that day from the store. Then at the last minute my job had called me and needed me for an emergency clean up, so I went straight to my job, leaving all my new makeup on my dresser, still in it's package's. But when I had returned I noticed right away that I had some item's missing, I even looked for my reciept to check what was missing, and the reciept was missing also. The expensive mascara that I purchased was replaced with some cheap mascara, it was still in it's original packaging but it wasn't the mascara that I had bought, this mascara was water proof, I don't use water proof mascara, it's too hard to get off at night. I was gone for a good four hour's and Alix must have came into my room while I was gone, and took the risk of taking my expensive makeup, then go a block away to the drugstore, changed my expensive makeup for cheaper makeup, since she must of had the reciept to, then kept the extra money that I had paid more for the better quality makeup and pocketed that. Those cheap item's were not the same expensive good quality item's I had bought. A couple of the makeup item's she kept because when I had caught her sneaking down the hallway the following day, I noticed her face was all done up and she had on some expensive eye shadow, the same color's I had originally purchased and some thick mascara, just like the kind I bought, it was like a deep shade of green mascara, I know that wasn't just coincidence to wear that color of mascara, and must of been why she was sneaking down the hallway, who know's what that biotch be up to. That also meant that she could hear what I say over the telephone to and what is said to me because she must have known that I was gonna be gone for those more than four hour's. She is a scrunja, and would do something like that, she wasn't slick and I figured it out, damn lowlife bitch! It wasn't too long after that incident that I moved out of the 'ol mansion anyway.

The 'ol mansion is so weird, and I never would have given first month's rent last month's rent and the three hundred dollar's deposit fee and moved into there if I would have known, but at that time I had no idea it would be scary and weird living there. Even the two guy's that lived in the room next to mine were weird. One night I kept real quiet in my room for about an hour, and I didn't have on my loud music as I usually did, I just wanted to see if I could find out anything around there. So after about an hour of keeping quiet with my light's out I opened the entrance door to my room real slowly and quietly I tip toed down the hallway and saw that those guy's door was open just a crack, it didn't look like anyone was in there, so I peeked inside and I saw many computer's, camera's with tv screen's in there, now what was that about, that made me very suspicious of the guy's next door. I heard the bathroom door behind me open up and just at that moment I began knocking on their door, to make it seem like I wasn't looking in there. One of the guy's came out of the bathroom and he looked real surprised to see me, I turned around to look at him and said; 'Hi, I just knocked on your door to ask if you have any sugar that I could borrow.' I needed an excuse so I used that one, he said 'no,' entered his room and closed and locked his door with a click behind him. That was weird they must be up to some heavy shit or something, I just didn't know what to think about it. It was then about ten in the evening at that time, I went back to my room and had my music jammed up loud for the rest of the night. Then the next day when I went to the community bathroom down the hall I had noticed that now those guy's next door room's door was wide open and empty. When I saw Burt later that day he told me that they had moved out real early that morning without telling anyone, and he had the nerve to call them weird. I hadn't bothered to tell him or anyone what I saw in their room the evening before.

So it was at that point I just said forget it, I started looking in the newspaper for aother place to live at even though I had paid a month in advance and a deposit, and they had my money. I just knew that I wouldn't be getting back any of my money I paid for the room, because of the dishonest manager, Burt, that lived next door to me in the dark apartment where he kept his curtain's closed 24-7, that right there is a sign of the man being a shady person and probably up to no damn good, I should have known better then. But of course, that doesn't mean all people that have their curtain's closed 24-7 is up to no good, maybe they just don't like too much light. Myself I like alot of light in the home. At first I hadn't noticed what a strange person Burt is, although I should have had an inkling about him when I had first answered the newspaper ad and walked up the flight's of stair's that night I came to look at the small room for rent. Burt must of had something in mind back then, because why did he ask me if I had a boyfriend or anyone that would be going in and out of the rented room other than me. I didn't think anything about it then, because that wasn't my nature to be suspicious, but it sure is now, after all I had started to experience around the creepy place's I rented and then had to live in. It's not easy to come up with the first and last month and deposit money for a place to live, and then get scarde out of it, and then have to come up with another two month's rent and deposit the very next two week's or month and then move again, bringing your own furniture with you and having to get a moving company to move you and pay them to and then it happen's all over again. Who were the darn pest's that kept bothering me, who was stalking me, who was is, I didn't know, yet.

That first night I had went to the ol' mansion to talk to the manager Burt about renting a room, it didn't look that bad to me, I had never had to live the way that I did, I mean living in a rented room, but for now I had to, and each time I found a place it turned out to be a nightmare, so I was so glad that I had the 'black room' at the police station to sleep in., it seemed to be my only safe haven there at the Oakland Police Headquarters where I worked in the maintenance department. When I answered the newspaper ad that Burt had put in there and I went to his room next door for him to show me the room, I should have known better then. Burt's leg was bleeding and he looked roughed up. He had told me that he got into a fight at the corner bar, and the guy he fought with pushed him into the juke box and that is how he cut his leg. Well I knew that going to some bar's will get you into a fight if you even look at the wrong person the wrong way, especially with him being a man and all. Really he didn't act like a mature man, even though he was in his thirty's. He acted like a big brat, so I refer to him as a real asshole that didn't act his age. Two day's after I moved into that hell hole, Burt knock's on my door and tell's me he will be out of town for a couple of day's. I think he just wanted to keep my money, scare me out of there and then have the next person pay more money, and do the same thing to them. Strange that when I first moved into there the front door on the first floor would alway's close and lock securely. Then a few day's later, the front door would not lock at all, and was stuck on unlocked from then on. Then a few day's after living there I had no electricity, everyone else in the entire building had electricity except me. I went without electricity for two day's, and at night only used candle's and the light that shown through the window's from the street light that hung above the window from the outside. Then I got the smart's and went out to the hallway and unpluged a cord that was going into Burt's room, since he had told me he wouldn't be home for a few day's, why would he need the electricity, I was there in my room and I needed the light. After those day's without electricity I went out to the hallway, unplugged the extension cord that ran under Burt's door into his room, and ran the cord into my room so that I could have some light. Burt was supposed to be out of town, and of course, he left no phone number for the owner's of that big drafty Ol' mansion so I couldn't call them for any maintenance problem's, like the electricity not working. But then it only took about twenty minute's from after I unplugged the electricity cord that went under his door so he could have electricity and led it into my room that Burt suddenly showed up and told me that the electricity should work now. I knew that right before I opened the door to him because I had accidently turned on the light switch that was right next to the front door.

"Why do you show up now, Burt, after all these day's I had to go without electricity and you were supposed to be out of town, all of a sudden your back! You weren't out of town, you were there all the time, weren't you."

"I was out of town." Burt replied with a smirk.

"Oh yea sure Burt, and now the light's are on after I had disconnect that extension cord that lead into your room for light and suddenly your back, yea sure. I never heard you coming up the stair's either."

"Can I have my extension cord back now?"

"Hold on, I'll bring it to you in a minute, it didn't work anyway."

"What, yes it did."

"How would you know you've been out of town, and when you get back the electricity is on. I'll bring the cord right over, hold on." He couldn't see that on the other side of the door I had the extension cord plugged in. But I just told him it didn't work because when I realized he was playing a real screwed up trick on me and making me go without electricity for all those day's well he made me mad. He just enjoy's messing with me so I'll mess with him, and see how he like's trick's played on him. Yea, all that time when I saw other people that lived in the ol' mansion they told me they had light, but I didn't.

I knocked on Burt's door and gave him back the electrical cord, "Here's your cord back that I tried to use for like twenty minutes, it don't work." Ha, if he even bother's to try it he will find out it does work, well that's what he get's for messing with me.

What a creep Burt is, alot of strange thing's would happen there. Like the first night that I had fell asleep there, I had my Cockatoo, Snoop's there with me, I had what seemed to be a bad nightmare, but now I began wondering that maybe it wasn't a nightmare, but what really happened. I was asleep, then suddenly I woke up for a couple of second's in the nightmare, and when I opened my eye's, I saw some thin rope's wrapped around my hand's like someone was using me as a puppet, as stranger's looked on, I couldn't stay awake and I fell back asleep, was that real?" What was happening, what kind of a cruel joke was this that was happening to me, what where they doing to me, who were they, I couldn't stay awake at that time, somehow they had drugged me, but with what and who?

Then there was the time when I had put fresh brand new sheet's, pillow sham's and bedspread on my new bed that I had just purchased from a furniture store. I wanted my own bed no matter where I lived at. I knew it was unusual to take my own bed from place to place everywhere I moved to, but I wanted to sleep in my own bed and not a bed that many has slept on. I had meant to put on the new bed spread set the day before but I had woke up late and had to rush off to work that morning, so I waited until I returned from work. The bed looked neat and the new bed spread set was made so good that you could bounce a dime off of it. I was then sitting back on a chair listening to music and sipping on beer, all by myself. I would often do that, and also dance to the music if I felt like it. Only that time I wanted to sit back and just kind of look around the room. The new crisp bedspread I had just fixed my bed with looked nice. But then the bedspread started to move and sag to one side. How could that be, just for some reason I had a strange feeling that maybe someone had sewn something alive into my bedspread set. It was a pretty bedspread and was quilted. No way this can't be happening, so I straightened it out again and sat back and watched as the quilt cover began to move again. So I pulled all the cover's off of the bed and just as I was gonna cut open the quilt to look at the inside, there was a knock at my door, I opened it and it was Burt. How strange, what timing, did he have a hidden camera somewhere planted in my room where he was watching me. Those were the day's before internet and camera phone's, the only thing I had was a pager.

"Hello AngeLoner, I don't even want to ask you, but would you low your music? I had been drinking all night and am tired today, say you got a beer?"

I set my open beer on top of the end table where my levi jacket was, by the open front door with Burt standing there.

"Yea, I got an extra beer." so I turned around and walked over to the small refrigerator grabbed Burt a cold one, then handed it to him. I shouldn't have given him a beer after the way he did me with the electricity, but because I am a nice person I did give him a beer.

"Yeaaa," he immediately pop's open the beer and begin's to gulp it down, then just kill's the can to the bottom. "Thank's, you got another one"?

I look up to him, he's a tall man. "Ah, no, go and buy your own, check you later." I close the door, and I can hear him dragging his big feet down the hallway to the top floor bathroom. I then lock my front door behind me, grab my beer from the top of the end table and drink down the rest of it, smash the beer can, throw it into the trash can and snap me open another, I just had suddenly became real thirsty and drink that one down. But then I felt a little drowsy, thus forgetting about the bedspread situation, I sat up in my bed, then some slow oldie music came on, and I was thinking, 'hey, I never did low the music for Burt and he couldn't have really cared less because he got him a beer and left. I layed back and passed out thinking, 'Oh no, that bastard Burt must have slipped something into my beer when he came to the door and my beer there, open accesible for him to slip something into it.....................I drifted off into a deep sleep, and that is what it felt like, that same familiar feeling of when........................

I feel deep into a kind of a sleep, but was still halfway awake and I started thinking back to year's before, when I let a boyfriend I had then named Amin live with me, when I owned a home in Hayward. Amin came home to me in the evening's after working all day at his own store in Oakland which was about twenty minutes away. He hadn't moved in any furniture or even any clothes, he had less than his basic's there, only a toothbrush, and a couple of extra t-shirt's, underwear, and one pair of jean's. He lived with me for one year, and during all that time he never paid me one penny for rent, food or anything. His excuse was that he didn't live there but just came there in the evening to sleep there, and that he didn't eat there either but ate at his store before coming back for the evening. He didn't mention that we spend all the week-end's together, and have sex. He was really my boyfriend but he wouldn't say it because he did not want a commitment. How could I have been so stupid to fall for his lie's, because in the end of our relationship, he finially told me the truth about what he was really up to. The day came when he told me that he was going to marry his Cousin whom had just come to America from Arabia, his family had set up the marriage between him and his Cousin, they do that mostly so their name will carry on in the future, I guess. Amin had been in America for a number of year's now, he had come from Yemen, and even had went there for one month to visit a few month's before. I had no idea even then what his plan's were for the future, and that his plan's didn't include me. The only thing he bought me back from Yemen was some 'cad'. Cad is a green like leaf that you chew on and it make's you high like your speeding, I know one thing about it, it sure is good. But after that I never had anymore, can't get it you know. Although I saw on the new's where someone was growing that Cad in their front yard, and actually didn't know what it was until the authorities discovered it and told that person to cut it down, so I guess it can grow in California. I've never seen the actual plant, maybe I'll look it up on the internet. It was pretty good though, and got me heck of high. I asked him if it was illegal to bring that from Arabia, he told me yea that it probably was but they don't really know about this intoxicating leaf at custom's and he got through with it. But imagine that as good as I was to him for that year, I mean letting him live at my home for free, thinking that just maybe we would have a future together and then he tell's me about his Cousin. If I had known that from the beginning he never would have gotten a second date with me. He told me about his Cousin one time about a week before the last day we were together, but we were both drunk at the time, and I thought that he was joking with me, and didn't even think twice about it the next day, little did I know he wasn't joking at all.

Then the day came when he came back after working all day at his store and he bought me back a bouquet of flower's and a box of chocolate's, the first thing's he ever bought me during that entire year together. Well except for weed, marijuanna, he alway's had some of that. After he gave me the flower's and chocolate's he tell's me that this would be the very last evening that we would ever be spending together. Amin, in his early twenties, and me in my late twenties, I had really fell for him, first of all his good look's attracted me, well at least I thought that he was attractive, maybe some women wouldn't find him attractive at all, with his black tight curly hair cut into an average hair cut, his black moustache, deep black eye's, with a slim line body and some muscle's, not a whole lot of muscle but enough to look good. He was from the middle east, and some women wouldn't like that to begin with. My mistake was that I didn't know when I got involved that alot of this kind of men usually marry their own kind. I also liked him because he liked to drink alcohol just like I do. Oh, yea he used to bring a couple of six pack's from his store too on most night's, but that's a far cry from paying rent. I had never went into his store to get free food, as a matter of fact I kept away from the store because he told me that his family wouldn't approve of me, and he had his Uncle working at his store, and his Uncle would call home to Yemen and tell his father everything he was up to, so I just stayed away from his store. But I'm still a young woman and I like my good time's, and to me partying like that is a real good time. Some women would want money, jewelry and whatever they can get in return for a relationship like Amin and I had, but I wasn't greedy, I really just wanted the truth from him, and real love, but all that time I had only gotten lies from him.

When he came home that evening with the box of chocolate's and the flower's at first I was so happy to recieve these two lovely gift's from the man I thought that I was in love with for a year. But thinking back now to how cheap he was, he had that good sized store and that's all he did for me all that time. Anyway, from the very beginning deep down inside I had a feeling that it wouldn't last between us, but I kept the hope that it would. Amin just wanted a place to sleep at night, a nice place to sleep at night and get some great sex too! That's also what I wanted, sex, but I also wanted a lasting relationship and real love to go with the sex.

I put the flower's in a nice vase of water, and set the box of chocolate's down on the cocktail table. We had a few beer's that I had chilled in my refrigerator, and he fired up a big fat joint. We were both feeling good from the effect's of the alcohol and drug's, then he broke the new's to me about marrying his Cousin, and by the way he looked at me told me that he wasn't joking around about it, and it was true.

"What are you for real, am I hearing right, you say that your gonna marry your Cousin? In America that's incest! How could you do this to me after all this time, you just used me, you liar, you cheater, you bastard!"

"No, he say's, I never cheated on you, I have never had sex with her yet, that will be after we get married."

"What, screw you, get out, get out of here, get out of my life!"

He stood up from the chair he thought that he was gonna get comfortable in for one more time, put on his leather jacket, and just like that he was gone out the front door. I grabbed the box of chocolate's and threw them at his car as he pulled out of the driveway. The box broke open and all the chocolate's fell on to the road way. I ran into the house to get the vase with the flower's in it and throw it at his car, but he had sped off too quick. I then threw the flower's outside into the garbage can.

I felt so hurt for how he had used me and lied to me for all that time, he had a year to waste out of his life, and decided to waste a year from my life too at the same time. Day's went by, I had spent alone in my house. I called in sick to work, sat back and drank. Beer after beer after beer, day after day after day. People would call me or come over and knock on my front door, but I didn't care, I didn't even answer the door or even the telephone. I had to get Amin out of my system, and that took day's. I would drink one day and chill the next day, then drink the next day and chill again. Finially Amin was out of my system. But to think he could just forget about me like that because he had somcone else, at that time I had no one else. I had cut all tie's with my friend's just like Amin had asked me to do, I shouldn't have done that, now I had nobody to party with, and I didn't screen my call's so I didn't even know who was trying to call. When I would hear a knock on the front door, I would either be real quite or turn up the music to drown out the sound of the knocking, I just didn't give a shit. I had saved up about thirty six-pack's of beer that Amin had brought back each night, those were the six-pack's that we hadn't drank, we didn't drink every night. But then he owned his own market, the Red Sea Food Market in Oakland. So the next day when he went off to work I would put the extra beer's into the garage and they all added up. I simply got the beer from the garage and then chilled it into my kitchen fridge and guzzled them down, jammed up the music, and danced all alone. Actually I had a blast all by myself. I fell asleep each night for only about a couple of hour's, then when I woke up, I took a shower then had a cup of coffee, and a t.v. dinner, that is what I did and lived off of for about a week. Then my telephone rang, I got tired of hearing it ring, and hadn't bothered to put on the answering service, but this time I did put it on and loud too. I could hear Amin's voice, he wasn't calling to apologize but instead asked me if he could give his good friend Bin, whom he also called the "Sheikh", my phone number. Just as I was about to pick up the phone and tell him to fuck off he had already hung up. Then an hour after, who call's but his friend 'Bin'. You would think that I had learned a lesson from Amin but no I hadn't, because Bin asked if he could come over and I told him okay. I gave him direction's on how to get to my home and he was there in an hour. Only when he got there he could barely speak any english, so I guess he had someone else talk for him over the telephone.

This man was also from the middle east, he wore a camouflage jacket over his clothes, and a white round hat, sort of like a turban only this hat didn't unravel. He was a very tall man with a black beard, kind of a long beard too, and black hair, with a dark complexion, and good teeth. He told me he was born in 1957. Bin was kind of good looking, but it was more the way he made me feel that attracted him to me. I alway's like the more soft spoken men with the dark black hair. it was that long beard I didn't care for too much. He seemed well educated too. But he drove a small car, I only knew that because I looked out of the window when he drove away a few time's alway's headed toward the back street's toward's Oakland I knew it was because going south he would have been driving to the freeway 880, but he never drove that way. When he came over I offered him a beer but he never drank a drop of the beer himself, however he did like whiskey. And when it came to alcohol and sex he understood english very well. Our mean's of communication was him watching me dance to the music, he love's the way I dance. I puffed away at some weed, but he didn't smoke any of that. But he did know some english and asked me if I am a American. I told him that I am Hawaiian, and automatically figured that he would know where Hawaii is and knew that I was American, but until this day I think that he thought I wasn't an American, and from some foreign country like he was. This man was very different from any other man that I had ever known, there was just something about him, I couldn't put my finger on it. He spoke alot in his language mostly, I guess it was Arabic or one of those language's, I don't know I couldn't understand it, only a very few word's that I had learned from Amin. Something told me that this man Bin is a very powerful man, just by the way he carried himself, I knew he held some kind of power. And he was sure smart enough to get into my pant's the first night we met, and every other time he came over we had sex. He would only stay for about three hour's each time, his mind is very powerful and each time he convinced me to have sex with him, and I gave into him. We never went anywhere together, I mean no where, but only stayed there at my place while I danced for him, we didn't communicate that well because he know's practically no english at all. He was very soft spokien, with a sort of soft voice, I never heard him raise his voice. He knew I used to train elephant's and care for elephant's, he liked that. He had even asked me, quite often if I wanted a million dollar's. I alway's told him "No", why would I take a million dollar's from him. Beside's I didn't really believe he had that kind of money, but who know's he probably did. It was kind of strange though, because I was into photography at that time, but just day's before my 35 mm camera was stolen, and I had made a police report on it too, so I never got to take a picture of Bin.

This man is strange and very different when he took off his clothes underneath them he had on those white thermal under clothes, the top's long sleeve and the long thermal bottom's, which he kept on even while we had sex. How strange, I never had that happen to me before with any other man, I mean keeping on the long sleeve thermal top, and the long john's too, however he did roll up his sleeve's, I noticed that he had one tattoo on his fore arm it was a small star, But was it a tattoo or a birth mark, anyway I didn't ask, and his beard would make me itch when he pressed up against my face. He alway's used a condom every time we had sex, not going out anywhere together was getting somewhat boring to me, but I just knew he would never take me anywhere. Anyway why was that, was he well known to other's, Oh, I just didn't know, we just stood at my home each time I danced and I drank beer, smoked weed and had sex with him, he drank some whiskey. I guess I knew that relationship wasn't gonna last, he was in my life and out of my life with in a few week's. This was about late 1981 to early 1982. I never got a photo of Bin because strangly enough my 35 mm camera had gotten stolen a week before I met him.

"AngeLoner, Angel, are you there?" I finially really woke up out of the cloudy thought's of the past, there was someone pounding on my door. I shook my head and felt like I was drugged, and knew instinctively that I was drugged, and Burt must have dropped something into my beer when I had it on the end table, and he stuck his nose into my room, damn bastard, what was he up to? The pounding on the door got louder and I could hear Burt outside my door arguing with someone, so I got up and opened the door, it was Oscar from the second floor.

"Whuz up Oscar, how you doing?"

"AngeLoner, could you ask your guest's not to knock so loud". Burt get's into Oscar's face and say's, "And that goes for you, Oscar!"

"Come on in Oscar", he walk's into my room, and I slam the door shut with Burt standing there. "He sure is an asshole, ain't he."

"Yea, ;he is, but what was he doing coming out of your room Angel?"

"What, are you sure, I was just passed out, and let me tell you what happened". I explained to Oscar about Burt possible dropping something into my drink. He said that sound's like something that Burt would do. I thought to myself, and then remembered my money that I had in my work pant's pocket laying next to my beer can that he must have spiked, and damn sure enough the money was gone.

"What's wrong AngeLoner?"

"My money I had in my work pant's is gone, and I know it was there before Burt came by. It was that damn Burt, he stold the money. I'm gonna go zap his ass, damn bastard thief!"

"Wait a minute AngeLoner, I'm gonna get Burt later anyway!"

"No, fuck that, I'm going there now"! I got my tazer gun, and planned to shock Burt real good. I went to his door and pounded on it, he wouldn't answer the door, damn freak. I mean there are freak's and there are freak's. Freak of nature is cool, but for a person to make himself a freak by the thing's he does is not cool at all.

I spoke to Burt through the door, "Burt, I know you stold my money, after you dropped some kind of drug into my beer, your a damn thief!"

I left the room and went into my room, shut and locked the door behind me, although locked door's don't seem to mean much around here. I kept real quiet because I knew that it would be just a matter of minute's before the police would be here to ask question's about all the noise. So if I kept quiet in my room maybe nobody would knock on my door.

I stuffed my pipe with some real good grade marijuanna, my back was hurting me from kicking on Burt's door, and the marijuanna help's ease the pain, yea, no fooling it does help. I sat back in the round shaped chair, and got me a cold one, glad that it was a twist on because I wouldn't want anyone from the other side of the door to hear me cracking open beer's. Because I wasn't about to open my door, if the Popo came knocking, I didn't care if they smelled the weed, after all there are plenty of other tenant's that could be smoking weed too, and they do, like stinking Burt. And now I could hear some heavy footstep's coming up the stair's, there was still enough sun outside to see. I wasn't trying to put my ear to the wall and hear what was being said next door, I could hear the muffled sounding deep voice's on the other side of the wall. No one knocked on my door though, so when I heard no sound out in the hallway, I peeped out the door. They were gone, or at least I thought they were then here's a knock at the door.

It was a police officer at the door that I had seen around the police station, "Yes sir, can I help you?"

"How are you, have you seen a man around here........

"A man? I haven't seen anyone unusual, why what happened?"

"Your neighbor got into a scuffle and........."

"Oh, that's ok sir, I don't want to know, my neighbor is alway's up to no good anyway. I haven't seen or heard nothing at all, I had fell asleep for awhile. Can I go now?"

"Oh sure, be careful around here now, take care."

Yea, thinking of my life, well I can settle for just drinking beer and puff's of weed. After all I do have a Cannibus Club card, because of the back pain I get sometime's but mostly my neck and shoulder be hurting real bad. I get pain from when I worked for the school district and they over worked me there by telling me to work through my first break at work and take a little longer lunch. Only by doing that, because I am so used to taking all my break's at work, that messed my arm's up sometime's and I can't lift anything heavy anymore, it's all painful most of the time. I had worked there full time a few year's ago, and for the first time in my work history I got hurt on the job, it had to go to worker's compensation, I never got a penny from it. All I got was the money paid back to me that I paid for my own medical coverage, which I had to keep because of the symptom's of carpal tunnel in my arm's. They even did surgery on both hand's for this, you can't tell at all. It sure was painful when they did the surgery on my hand's, and I was awake all the time, but the school district couldn't care less about it and like I said never compensated me for lost of wage's, no not one penny, that sure is cold huh, I mean about nobody caring about me getting hurt on the job. Then after awhile I was supposed to go on disability, heck I don't want to go on no disability and be disabled because of the pain I get when doing to much lifting, so I came back to work for the City. But I still have to pay over three hundred dollar's a month for medical coverage because the City doesn't have any benefit's for part timer's, I have to pay for my own, and I do want the very best coverage I can get. That and paying for the different dive's I have to live in take's up all my money. I stay so busy that I don't have time to look for a better job."

I looked out the bay window to the officer's car below, he was writing out a report, then suddenly he started up his siren and took off.

CHAPTER THREE

DEALING WITH THE UNKNOWN

Now I still had to deal with the blanket & bed spread's, and what was making the bedspread's move, I went over to the bed, took my buck knife and cut the bedspread open on the edge of it. 'Oh shit!'. there were little live snake's sewn into the outer edge of the bed spread, and that is what made the bedspread's move when the snake's moved. But who in the heck was doing this to me, and why? Who was sneaking into my room and who is crazy enough to do this, it's insane, it has to be some crazy ass person, and a very weird one to do this. I had just purchased that new bedspread the week before. I just had a bad feeling that Burt was in on it, that did it for me, I had to get out of the ol' mansion and soon. I had even noticed that a couple of my blue jean's that had fit me real good, and made my ass look extra shapely, I noticed that I had and used for over a year already now was too big for me. Then when I looked at the jean's closer I noticed that someone had switched them to a larger size, they were the original levi's and wouldn't be hard to find a bigger size to switch them with. That's some crazy stuff, done by a person that's very jealous of me. Then I remembered about Alix, the woman that would often be at Burt's next door, as she would visit him and stay with him for a few day's at a time every now and then. I thought of when she showed me some of the thing's that she had sewn, and how handy she is with a sewing needle.

And how when Alix had came to my room to beg for a couple of dollar's to catch the bus to pick up her county aid check, and how Snoop's had acted when he saw her, he screeched so loud in distress when he saw her, now that's telling me something. I know my Cockatoo and if she had never seen her before she wouldn't have screeched so loud. She must be one of the people sneaking into my room when I am gone, and she must be the one who had sewn the snake's into my bedspread and switched my jean's, not to mention I had some nice clothes missing. Now who do she think she is to do those thing's to me, I have never done anything to her, and really barely knew her, what a nut she is, I know it's her, is she doing these thing's on her own, no she must be in it with Burt. Maybe someone is paying them to mess with me, but who, and why? And was there other's too, I had to find out. Well before I move out of this ol' mansion, I'm gonna go and find that bitch and whip her ass for what she did, but I will have to find out for sure first, but I will find out even if I have to beat it out of that damn bitch. Just then Snoop's started to screech real loud, he could sense something, so I opened the door to my room, and snap, look who is standing out there, ha, it was Alix, she was out there I caught her trying to peep through the door key hole just as I opened the door. Snoop's was screeching so loud that I stepped out the door into the hallway.

"So what's up Alix?" As I look at her I notice that she had on some thick mascara on her lashes, and thinking to myself, "Hah, I wonder if that is the brand new mascara that I'm missing".

"AngeLoner, do ya knew whare Burt is, he's frent dor brek don, and he nat ther."

I acted like nothing was the matter, you know with the bedspread and my blue jean's and other thing's going on. I told her, "No, I don't know anything about that, accept the Popo was her, asking question's, and I told them the same thing, I know nothing".

"Why hes frent dor brek down?" Alix asked, in her ilterate word's.

I told her that I didn't know, she is nothing but a bitch and snitch anyway, and alway's up to no good. So I walked down the hallway and took a look at Burt's door. "Let's see, oh yea, his door sure is broken down huh. Well someone must have been real pissed off at him, he need's to stop messing over people." We entered Bart's studio, at least he had a kitchen there with a small stove and fridge, more than I had in my tiny studio. We started to look around, and I noticed Alix's sewing can, left open sitting on a end table. "You sure can sew can't you Alix?"

She then ran across the room to cover the sewing can that I was looking into, because i wanted to see if the thread matched up with the thread sewed into my bedspread. Sure enough it was the same kind of orange thread. I grabbed her by her butterfly collar, and shook her, "You damn bitch, you better tell me now if your the person that sewed those small snake's into my new bedspread, it's the same orange thread, you damn bitch, I'll kick your ass!"

And believe me I could really kick ass, there's one karate punch I would practice doing. I could even punch a brick wall so hard without cutting or my knuckles bleeding. Being quick and precise at it.

I never got nothing out of her, but it must of been her. I walked out of Burt's stinky, smelly place, and tried slamming the door, only when I did that the entire door fell off it's hinge's. Went back to my room, sat on the chair, fired up a fat joint and had a cold beer, blasted the music and I was angry. Angry for the envasion of my privacy and what the creep's all around me was pulling on me. I yanked all the bed cover's off of the bed, I would never use them again. I was just so tired of these weird-o's messing with me behind my back, especially since I hadn't done anything to them for them to do these thing's to me.

I went back into my room, and slammed the door as hard as I could, my clothes hanger holder fell off of the back of the door, then punched my tightened fist right into the hard wood door, putting a crack into it. I often practiced my karate punch on solid wood. Alix was very lucky that I didn't bitch slapped her and that I didn't hit her with my karate punch. If most people hit a hard surface like that bare handed they would break there hand or arm doing it. But not me I had been doing that for year's, thinking someday I may need to use that hit in an emergency, an emergency to protect myself. I hung the clothes back on to the door.

Oscar knocked on my door, stepping inside he asked me what were all the leaves doing on my floor.

I use them for the fresh outdoor kind of minty smell they have to them." Actually the leaves were there to keep giant ant's away, but I didn't feel like having to explain about all of that right now.

"What the heck, look up there at the ceiling Angel."

"Where, up at the attic, I know I tried to cover that hole in the ceiling put the card board I put up there just fell back off."

"You know I get the feeling someone is watching me, I just wonder if there are any hidden camera's around here. Because I know someone has been watching me and entering my room when I am not here, and also at night when I am sleeping. So when I do sleep here, I sleep with all my clothes on, and now I have Snoop's to watch my back, but I can't always's depend on the bird to awaken me if someone come's in here when I am asleep because sometime's I fall into a deep sleep. I have heard somewhere about people being into a deep realm of sleep and that during fifteen to twenty minute's while a person is asleep that they can't awaken to any noise. On some morning's when I had even awaken the next morning a few time's I could smell the distinct smell of ether on me. Like maybe someone entered my room while I was in one of those deep sleep's then immediately put a rag with ether on it to keep me asleep. I have even found these three small marking's on my arm's mostly upon awakening in the morning's. I don't know what these mark's are from, and they are alway's in three's, like point's to a pyramid, I have about four different set's of marking's on me."

"Let me see AngeLoner." I show Oscar the mark's on my arm's.

"Well, do they hurt, they don't look like much, but yes, where would those marking's come from, gee, I just don't know. Honestly I never knew about all this, after all I have never spied on you. Now I'm very concerned about all of this, after all we are friend's, and I care about you my friend.

"I'm glad that now I have someone on my side, I mean to help me to catch whoever is doing this to me. And I know where you can start checking this out at. I think that Burt next door just may know something about this, but I can't say for sure.

I told Oscar about what had happened, even about the snake's sewed into the bedspread, and how I busted Alix.

"It's not safe for you to live here, AngeLoner."

"Oscar, your right, it never was safe for me to live here to begin with and that is why I didn't want you to know where I lived at. I'm sure that no one would believe me about what goes on around here, I mean I have alway's had a feeling that somebody's watching me. A short while back the popo came here because Burt claimed he got burgularized, so when they knocked on my door to ask me if I had seen anything out of the ordinary, I told them no, I hadn't seen anything, buy could they check out my room because there's snake's in my room, that was even before I discovered the small live snake's sewn into my bedspread. But I know there has been big snake's here too! When I told the officer that he looked at me sideway's, like I didn't know what I was talking about or something, so I told him to look under the bed and there was some snake shit under there. I know what snake shit look's like because when I had worked at a zoo for eight year's and took care of a few snake's there when the regular employee went on vacation, I filled in for him to care for the cold blooded animal's. I had swept under my bed two day's before that, so that shit had to have been from recently. The officer then looked under my bed, see's the shit, pull's a small plastic baggie out of his front top pocket, put's the shit into the plastic baggie and told me that he was gonna have it analyzed. Now can you believe that. I had the officer's name and I even called him a couple of time's at the station to ask him what the result's were, but he was never in his office and he never returned my call's either. I think that maybe he was faking it and that he never had that snake shit analyzed, he never really cared about it anyway. Oe heck just maybe he found out what it was and didn't tell me. I've heard that when people complain about snake's that for some reason the F.B.I. is supposed to investigate, I wonder if that's true or not?"

"Yea, Oscar say's, I have read something about that being true but I have never encountered that problem myself. I do know about that one, I mean when an officer tell's you that they will check out whatever, and they hardly ever do. They just make out a report sometime's, as a mater of fact for every call an officer get's, especially in the big cities they are supposed to at least fill out a complaint card and turn it in daily, but alot of time's they don't even bother to do that, and report's either for that matter. They usually just get too busy on someday's when call after call come's in. I hadn't told you this before AngeLoner but I used to be a police officer".

"Wow, Oscar, really, heavy".

"But, please I don't want to talk about why I am no longer a police officer". You know nowaday's nearly everything that happen's end's up on You Tube, and sometime's thing's aren't alway's what they look to be. AngeLoner, what was that officer's name?"

"Well, I threw away his number, after I tried calling him to get the result's of that crap, he probably never bothered to have it analyzed.." I do remember he was oriental and wore glasses, and maybe in his thirty's?"

"Yea, sound's like him, how did you guess?"

"Well sweetheart, I know this beat and just about every officer that work's it. Just forget about that shit, your right he probably didn't bother to have it analyzed. I am concerned about you AngeLoner, I don't want anything to happen to you living here in this 'ol mansion. Haven't you ever been afraid to stay here? And why in the world didn't you ever mention any of this to me anyway? I want you to know that I am a friend".

"Mention it to you, how would I begin to even explain all this weird shit going on here, let me put it this way, since I realized about all these weird and dangerous game's around here, I have been sleeping at the police station, yep right there where I work at, there's everything one may need there anyway. A place to sleep at, work at, private restroom's, and vending machine's or snack bar to eat at, and when you go to the roof top there's quite a view of the city, the bay and both bridge's, even the Golden Gate can be seen from up there. I stood up there before and watched as they trained some of the recruit's on the top of the roof to the building across the street from there. Then I found out about the blackroom and how it has been a safe haven for me when I need a safe place to sleep at night. And not because of anything I ever did to anyone in my life, least they deserved it, it was all small time. I never burnt anyone for any thing, and I don't like to brag, but the truth is I cross no one's path. Can you dig it, I am just not that type. I stay to be a true friend, and is much easier to do now than when I first became an adult. But I don't want to get into that right now".

"My life is a busy life, and I really haven't taken as much time as I should for a personel life. But I do have time for a friend like you, right?"

"Yea, that's cool, Oscar".

"I want to know about something, what, where and how have you ever slept at the police station?"

"Well you see here where I live at now and how it is, with a bunch of creep's sneaking around here. So many night's I have needed a good sleep and I knew I couldn't get a good rest here. Then one day as I was working I had mentioned to a co-worker, that I don't even feel safe sleeping at my rented room in the 'Ol mansion, and he suggested to me that if I needed a place to sleep and had no where else to go because I didn't feel safe that I could sleep there, in the black room."

Oscar look's at me, shake's his head in almost disbelief and ask's, "The black room?"

"Yea. that's a room right down the hallway from where we punch in at the time clock for the day and where we have our office for the custodian's. Co-Worker told me one day that if I ever needed a safe place to sleep, that I could sleep there in the black rrom. Only he didn't call it the black room, I call it that. He's never had to sleep in there, so he wouldn't know what it's like to have to actually sleep in there, and be quiet in there, because I don't think the City would want me to make it a habit to sleep in that room, but I had no choice. Living alone, being alone, and working only my part time custodian job, well it is hard to pay for motel's, it get's expensive after awhile. That's just the life style that I got into, by working only part time. I've slept in the black room for so many night's because everytime I find a place to rent in this area, it alway's turn's spooky, it's like a damn demon is following me or something, trying to continually scare me and rip me off. But I knew that it would be safe to sleep in the 'black room' it's so dark in there. I don't turn on the light's because I don't want anyone catching me asleep in there, I use my custodian light key to turn off the light switch right next to the entrance door just in case anyone came in there, they wouldn't be able to turn on the light and then go to the next room down where the light's will go on."

"Oh, I know the two room's that you are talking about, where police officer's can sleep if they get tired and are working a extra long shift and may need a nap, the room's down the hall from where you work from in the basement."

"Yea, those room's, making sure the main light switch is turned off in one room has worked for me because there aren't any officer's that carry around a light key with them on their key chain's, so they don't think anything about it. A few time's I had been laying there on a lower bunk bed and someone had opened the door, of course you can't see to the back of the room where other bunk bed's in front of the bunk I'm in hide's the view. So when they go to turn on the light it doesn't go on, then they simply go to the other room where the light does work. Is that slick or what. Haaaahahha. If you've ever been in there then you know that there are no window's in there so it is pitch black in there, thus I call it the 'black room'. It's so dark in the room, especially when I first started to sleep in there, then someone put a lighted alarm clock in there, and now there is even a telephone in there, which I had used only one time, then there is the three set's of bunk bed's in there. I don't sleep under the bed spread's on the bunk bed's in there, but I just sleep on top of them, fully clothed except for sometime's I take my shoe's off to be a little comfortable. I usually sleep on the same bunk bed because some of the other bed's smell a little funky from someone else sleeping there. So when I am scheduled to clean the basement, I go into there and prop the door open and strip the bed I sleep on then wash the bed spread and sheet's in the washer and dry them in the dryer that we have in the custodian main supply room, plus at the same time I air the room out, as that is a part of my job sometime's anyway. So the door's to both of the room's are alway's kept locked anyway's, and most of the police officer's don't have the key to those door's anyway, it is a master key and they don't just hand those key's out to everybody. Which I alway's seen as a security breach to the police department, I mean for the Custodial Supervisor to hand out the master key to custodian's. But I know they knew that I could be trusted. But really they would just hang all the key's, even the key's to the back door of the police department, which was a big weird key. But that is how I would go to work in the early morning's. Beside's I can't speak for any other employee but I was very protective of my work key's, I had always' been that way even when I worked at the Zoo and cared for many dangerous animal's. And caring for those animal's, a Zoo Keeper has the key to their night houses because those night houses has to be cleaned every day. Mostly hosed down into a water trap that would trap any left over bone's, or food even dung goes into that water drain that had a screen. I hated to have to lean down and pull that darn trap out to dump and reclean it. But my friend that is another story of my real Zoo Stories, and boy do I have those true stories. check out one of my next book on that.

Although it does surprise me how the supervisor's trust people with the master key, I mean what if they hired a 'bad' custodian who is there just to spy or something and then handed out a master key to do their daily cleaning, because there are alot of part timer's there that just come and go, because they don't keep their job's doing part time work for to long because they want a full time position, and there is a long civil service list for those position's that offer a full benefit package. When I worked for the City of Berkeley at the City Hall, I even had the key to the Mayor's office, then any janitor there whom has that key and is scheduled to work in that area at night when there is nobody around can get real nosy and never be suspected. Darn, if I was a supervisor there I would take all those security measure's, which is so important. I have personally seen Custodian's go into office's and the first thing they do is open an empolyee's desk drawer and take all their change or whatever was wanted in there. But oh no, not me I have never been that way, my Mama brought me up right to respect other people's property. But heck I knew of some Supervisor Custodian's who did shit, so I just kept to myself and shut my mouth, till this day, mum's the word. So if I were a Supervisor there I would not let any part timer's use the master key, and I would have all employee's, including Janitor's and Custodian's, especially have background check's. They never did that in those day's, and I don't know if they do it today. remember here I am talking about the early 1990's. Well except for the City of Berkeley, I had worked there from 1997 to 2000.

Even though everyone who work's there has their finger print's and any police record's checked out, you know like even for any driving ticket's they may have had, I still wouldn't trust them, what about their real criminal history. I have no felony's on my record, I have stayed clean all my life, well beside's driving ticket's, but then who don't have those in their past. But then I have root's with the City of Oakland and have for over ten year's experience with the City including from when I worked at the Oakland Zoo from 1975 to 1983. It wasn't alway's steady I had taken off when I was pregnant, and a few other time's. But then I had been going to the Oakland Zoo since I was about five year's of age. It's a very long story.

I used to have my picture in the newspaper all the time when I helped to train elephant's, it was alot of hard work, but fun for me and the elephant's. A young elephant is called a punk. What I hate is when animal right's people talk about it is cruel and mean to train elephant's, and use chain's and hook's. Well they are wrong and they don't know what they are talking about, and only what they think they see. A elephant hook which is really called a 'teather' is only used to guide a trained elephant, and not made to hurt them. Could you imagine that if a elephant want's too that they could simply grab the teather out of a trainer's or handler's hand's break it in half and smash the person to death, and believe me that has happened. Sadly so I have known of that to happen to one person, and heard of it happening to other's, so don't be saying a person can be cruel to an elephant, they don't know what their looking at, and someone whom does mistreat a elephant or any other animal will get their's in the end. You know like getting smashed to death by an elephant or getting maimed or hurt by one, but I have never heard of that happening to a professional person that is very careful and take's precaution's, and have love for their elephant's. But also I'm sure innocent people have gotten hurt or killed by many animal's just by simply being there or in the way. So why put all the blame on elephant trainer's. I know what it is about people that complain about trained elephant's, because I know of quite a few people that has tried to train elephant's and are either hurt in the process of trying to train an elephant or for not taking simple safety precaution's and then become too frightened to get close to an elephant by themselve's ever again. Or they have failed in training elephant's because once the elephant get's big enough to knock them around, and they can no longer have the little elephant, which by now has began growing large, they can no longer have the elephant follow them around because of them perhap's holding a milk bottle for them and they won't follow them for a walk anymore, they give up and so they can't train elephant's, because they just don't know how, then they give up on the idea of training elephant's and turn to 'animal right's', which turn's out to be 'animal wrong's' because they don't know what they are talking about when it come's to training elephant's because many have failed at trying to train an elephant themselves and therefore are jealous of the elephant trainer and even the trained elephant. Chaining elephant's up at night time is just like putting a baby into a play pen, and that is not cruel. But elephant's should never be chained up all day and all night, that would be cruel. Trained elephant's should be taken for walk's and excercise every day starting at early in the morning then put into a good sized space where they can move around in, something like the way horses have a corral. If I were an elephant I would love to take walk's everyday, and go to carnival's and the beach, birthday parties and parades. In the wild elephant's are being slaughtered for their precious ivory. Our only hope is Elephant Trainer's and Zoo's. And of course the many Mahout's that work, eat, live and sleep right along next to their beloved elephant, the Mahout usually grow's up with their elephant with the both of them being very young to start off. Elephant's have been trained for thousand's of year's, I do believe this is why they are not extinct today, and the last to survive will be the elephant's that have trainer's or Mahout's.

I'm surprised that 'animal right's' people don't complain about horses with the bit's that are used in their mouth or the whip'sand spur's that are used to kick their heel's into the horses for them to run or move. When the elephant's are chained in the evening's, the ankle's get switched over every night never using the same ankle's two day's in a row. The trained elephant gladly put's his foot up to be chained for the evening, there is nothing wrong with that. Helping in working with elephant's for year's I have never seen a elephant abused, never! Even I saw on the new's before where they had film of a handler in the circus that was walking a elephant and guiding it with a elephant teather, and the media was saying that people complain about that being cruel, they had a woman on the new's that work's at a zoo, I won't say where the zoo is because I know who that woman is. But they had her on television and asked her if she thought how the handler in the circus was walking one of the elephant's and using a teather to guide the elephant, they asked her if she thought that was cruel. I guess they thought that she was an authority on elephant's because she work's at a zoo and around the elephant's there. She said that was cruel, when it was not cruel, I saw the same film. I know the woman that said that, and have heard about that woman and how alot of people that are professional's at training elephant's think's she is 'kooky' because they heard her speak at certain meeting's, and she talk's all crazy and don't know anything about what she's talking about when it come's to elephant's at all. This is because she's tried to train elephant's and failed and even became permanently maimed for life by an elephant, so now she speak's against trained elephant's because of what happened to her. She also got her job by lieing on her resume, said she had year's of experience training elephant's, so after some time of being around the elephant's where she got the new job, the professional elephant trainer noticed that 'she' really didn't know anything about elephant's, not even their diet's. So he called her reference on her job application and found out that she was lieing, the only experience with elephant's she had was shoveling up road apple's. By that time the professional elephant trainer whom was also her

Supervisor, did not want to fire her because he felt sorry for her because she had a finger digit swiped off accidently by one of the elephant's all because that woman lied on her job application about having experience working with elephant's when she had no experience because if she did she would have known how to stand around elephant's and also she did not listen to the professional trainer and what he warned her about from day one on being around elephant's. I know this to be true because I worked with that same professional elephant triainer for year's and I listened to his warning's about the danger's of being around the huge pacyderm's, I listened and thank goodnes I listened because I had never gotten hurt by an elephant, and neither did the professional trainer. But that trainer, he was so good with his trained elephant's, they loved him alot and he loved them alot too. He had the best breeding elephant 's in the United States before he retired, well into his 70's. Five of the female elephant's were pregnant from the male trained elephant. But the trainer retired and was not there for the birth's of the elephants', he alway's hoped the Zoo would hire a professional elephant to help with the elephant birth's. But he had left that woman in charge of the elephant's, and before he retired he made sure that the trained elephant's had a big new wonderful spacious elephant set. However because the professional elephant trainer retired and was not there for the elephant birth's, but that woman was there, and because she lied on her resume and really didn't know anything about training elephant's, none of the baby elephant's that were born survived.

One lasted over a year but without the knowledge of a professional trainer that baby elephant died too. I was watching the birth of one of the baby elephant's on TV one night and I couldn't believe my eye's, after one of the baby elephant's was born they had put the newborn into a hoist sling to move the newborn punk. I knew as soon as I saw that, that the baby elephant would have broken rib's. And sure enough later that's what they found out happened, broken rib's. People must understand we need elephant trainer's for our elephant's of today if we want them to survive. So many people are giving their opinion when they know nothing about elephant's period, only what they read or think they see on video's and not through year's of experience. Please support trained elephant's and elephant trainer's if you want our elephant's to survive through time.

So a person has to be careful even while just being around the giant mammal's. The only reason I am bringing all this up about 'that woman', is because of people like her that know nothing about how trained elephant's are really cared for and loved. I know she talk's hecka crap about me, and Trainer's I respect, so there! Anyway every elephant that has been born there, that if she really knew something about elephant's, they would have all survived. Just for her to care about herself, and not the requirements of the position is so selfish. Even this prove's that we need elephant trainer's for today, because with hand's on experience a trainer know's how to help with an elephant's birth. I'll say it again and again, if she knew a inkling about elephant's, all of those newborn elephant's would have survived. Too bad she had to lie on her job application, and the elephant's paid real bad for her lie's. The real professional elephant trainer was hoping they would hire a professional elephant person that know's about elephant's after he retired, but they never have til this day. That woman just get's job's for her family member's and let's them be in charge of the elephant's when they've had no previous experience, they do stay away from the elephant's, on the other side of a big heavy fence, and they say they are elephant trainer's because they command the elephant to lift their foot, while the elephant's that are there had already been trained before they got there and one elephant that I helped train is still there. The male elephant died while under 'that woman's' care, because I heard she let him eat Oleander plant's. That is very poisonous to elephant's. If she knew about elephant's and didn't change their diet the professional had them on well that male elephant would still be alive too. What a mess. For pete's sake get a professional elephant person to that Zoo.

JEWEL OF OAKLAND

Riding my bicycle into the cool fresh air of the early morning give's me a lift of spirit's just peddling around the Jewel of Oakland, Lake Merrit, and even getting good excercise felt good. My bicycle is a "Trek" brand and red in color, I just love to ride it because the ride is actually so smooth that it remind's me of steering a car, and sometime's forgetting I'm riding it and I find myself reaching for a blinker switch before turning a corner, I love riding a bicycle! When I get on to a country road riding, I just peddle with my eye's closed for a hundred feet or so, open them again to check the wide road ahead then because I know that the road ahead is wide and level, I ride another hundred feet or so. It's fun and great excercise, even riding and not holding on to the handle bar's, with my hand's on my hip's getting even more excercise as I turn from side to side in a twisting fashion keep's my waist at 26 inches. Now I'm not bragging but when I ride my bicycle or even go walking alone, I get alot of whistle's from men that I pass by.

Once I didn't know whether to smile or be mad at one construction worker that held up a piece of large cardboard as I walked by and he showed me the carboard from afar. First the cardboard had the number 6 written on it then he turned it over and it had the number 9 written on it. He point's at the number nine at first, I guess meaning that I was a number 9 on a 1-10. scale. Then he show's the number 6 and the number 9 again. You know like the number 69 when it is put together. And you know what the number 69 stand's for, it stand's for sucking each other off. Nasty guy, I flipped him off and kept walking to my job at he City police station to get my payroll check.

I've never had a problem in meeting a man, the problem has alway's been meeting a 'good man'. Purposely. often I dress in baggy levi's, but then that also was the fashion in the early 1990's, I also sometime's wear a hat or baseball cap and wear one of my favorite levi jacket's with the baggy pant's because the jacket cover's my shapely body and that way I don't need to deal with men trying to pick me up. I know that most probably most women love attention, and that's nice, I love attention too, but not from stranger's as we pass each other. Heck I've even had some women turn their head's to look at me, but I'm not that way. I know a few gay people and have no problem hanging out with them.

By the time that I got to the custodian department that is located in the basement of the City police station, I was way early and none of the other custodian's was there yet, the office phone was ringing, so I used my issued key's, unlocked the office door and answered the ringing, "Hello, custodian department, AngeLoner speaking."

"Goude moning, GanghaLoner, this Tom."

"Yes, how you doing, and that's A-N-G-E-L-O-N-E-R, not G-A-N-J-A-Loner, aren't you supposed to be here working with me today?"

"Yee, Anja, I shoo worka wih u toody, butta it a holladay. They calla me ande mak me worka ga ta corp yarda tooday."

"Oh wow, I forgot it's Memorial day, well I guess I will be working alone today then?"

"Yessa."

"So I dump your trash for you today then right Tom?"

"Ya, ya, ci u layta Gangha".

"Ok, I'll see you later, oh and Tom, I'm gonna teach you yet how to pronounce my name correctly, ok?"

"Oh, ya, ya, u helpah me telk betta, thet's goo no? Yessa thet's veddy goo."

Whew, I wonder where Tom got his accent from, it sound's like he has a little mixture of some other kind of accent too that he must have picked up on somewhere else. I alway's so much respect the fact that many people from other countrie's speak their language and also english, that's great, and gotta give them alot of credit for that. Heck, I'm glad they get to get a legit driver's license now, why not, what's the problem with that. Plus this bring's money to our country, for them to pay for their license and have car insurance, that show;s responsibility. Tom is very sweet though, and keep's alot to himself. I'm glad for him for that because most people don't like nosy people anyway, I sure don't. You know like people that mind's everyone's business except there own, and it is never for a good reason either but just to be nosy and to see what dirt they can pick up on a person. So that meant for today I would be working by myself because of the holiday all the other custodian's got the day off and the full timer's with pay, for us part timer's nothing just time and a half pay. I clocked in, exited the office, and locked the door behind me. Because the actual way it was set up in the basement that anyone could just wander into there, from off the street and wander into the office, if no one was around, and maybe steal something, or even a set of key's, although the key's are locked in a box, and not easy to get to, sometime's employee's leave the box open and unlocked, just like the trash gate outside. I don't know if they are just plain stupid, or lazy or even care about security. Because you just don't know who could be around there were no security door's at all from once you got on to the elevator to the office. Because I would be responsible and I am a responsible person anyway's, I knew to keep the office door closed and locked if no one else was around. Some of the other worker's didn't give a darn much about security and left the office door open when no one was around and they had to just go to another floor, they are just too lazy to lock the door for that short of a time, because they wouldn't want to have to unlock it again, it only take's a few second's for them to steal, seriously there are people that are that lazy.

And since I had to do my job and his, that meant I just had to empty all the trash can's and nothing else, since I was doing the work of two people today, and in a way that make's it easier when working alone anyway. That is the way the supervisor told us custodian's to do it, that is, when we have to do our work and someone else's for the day. And of course, clean up any emergency spill's too, like if I'm working on the fourth floor and I get a call over the radio to clean a coffee spill on the first floor or something like that, so I had to be around and not just do my job and leave. Unless it's after noon time, we were allowed to leave after twelve thirty noon if we got everything done by then. Some custodian's just knock out emptying the trash in a couple of hour's and then split for the day, and they get paid for the whole day and get away with it too.

I knocked out my duty's that day extra fast, like the 'clean up woman', ever heard that song, it's cool.

I time myself well when I work, taking my fifteen minute break's on time and lunch's too. But like alot of us did if we finish early we would go sit in some empty room to kill time because we aren't allowed to leave early, at least some of us aren't, at least not on a daily basis. Well never the less the rule's are tight at the police station especially on week day's and really not that lax. Just as I get into the office and ready for lunch, as I usually alway's ate lunch before leaving for the day, the telephone ring's, it might be important I better answer it. The voice on the other side is Henry the week-end supervisor.

"AngeLoner, how you doing, this is Henry."

"Hi Henry, what is it?" I played around so much with the many men out there that flirted with me, only the men that I desired I welcomed, but the men I adored from afar, I could never get with. There is two working main supervisor's for the City of Oakland custodian's, one is for the park's and recreation department and the other is for public work's. Henry is one of the supervisor's that I had sex with while we were both on duty. I never told anyone about it, but I had a feeling after Henry and I was together having sex that the gardner's were watching us through a side window, because a couple of day's later while I was sitting in the gym reading a book, during my break at the same time Henry and I had sex day's before, I caught a gardner peeping through a side window. I got up and ran to the window and asked him what was he looking for, I noticed that both of the gardner's were peering through the window, and they didn't say anything but just walked away with a big smile on their faces. That was sort of telling me something, and I sure didn't appreciate that, I mean someone, anyone spying on us like that. I had sex with Henry that day, because he turned me on alot and we were alone there, at least supposed to be alone there, beside's I didn't know that Henry's married, or I wouldn't have been with him in the first place, he sure doesn't wear a wedding ring. I didn't want anyone to know about what we did that cold winter morning. It was embarrasing, not to mention that the both of us would be written up. But then I didn't really care about being written up, after all the custodian job offered me no benefit's, and not enough hour's of work either, all it did was pay well enough to pay my bill's, and that was it. Then on the other hand, Henry had everything to lose if they found out about him, because he's a supervisor, with high pay and full benefit's, he had everything to lose. I just found Henry to be a sexy man, even though he was missing a couple of finger's, I never asked him how it happened, and I didn't pay attention to it, since he alway's wore black leather gloves, even when we had sex, he had his gloves on. But I had seen him take off his gloves once to wipe off the glove's when he had gotten some amonia on them. Henry has a loud personality, and a big, well you know what. It just happened that morning, one time. When I got to work early that morning there was a alarm going off inside the building, it was a low sounding alarm and couldn't be heard from outside the building, but I could hear it from inside the building and thought that maybe it is important. I worked there alone in the building from six a.m.

until ten a.m., and so that morning the low beeping sound, that I thought was a alarm, was going off, so of course, what does one do when that happen's, I called my supervisor Henry and told him about the annoying sound. He came to my job site, fixed two problem's, first he turned off the low beeping sound, I couldn't figure out how to turn it off, and at first he couldn't either, but then he figured it out. Then secondly fixed the problem that we were both there alone and both horny.

Henry climaxed so fast that day, he pushed him self deeper into me, to be sure that I was also fully satisfied, and I was too, for that day. Then after a few day's I found out that Henry is married, oh snap, I made sure it would be a one time thing, I don't like messing with married men period, he got to me on the sly.

Henry realized that I wasn't gonna give in to him again when he had me alone in a supply room a couple of week's after that at the Corporation Yard, when I was there getting supply's. As I work all over the city of Oakland and was not assigned to one place for too long. Many of the custodian's was there that morning as Henry gave out the supply's that is needed to replenish the supply's that are needed at work, like boxes of paper towel's, toilet paper, cleaning liquid's, just what ever is needed we get and record it down on the work sheet. Henry handed out everyone's needed supply's and saved me for last to give me my supply's. I knew what he was up to there in the supply room when we were left all alone. He tried to get me to suck him off, right there in the privacy of the portable supply room.

'Oh heck no, I ain't doing it,' I thought to myself. Also the xupply boxes were stacked in a way that there could have been someone hiding beind them to watch us. Even though I've been through a couple of thousand boyfriend's, and have experienced all that sex, I have only sucked on five different men throughout my sex life, and those men were my favorite men that I have been with. "No", I told Henry these lip's of mine is not touching you right there, in that spot, so forget it, beside's I found out that your married!"

"What does that have to do with this, I can even give you more work hour's and transfer you to a cozy spot."

"No, no, no, I had sex with you because I find you sexy, and you felt good, I even thought that we could get something going on with each other, you know like a actual relationship. But now that I know that you are married, forget it, that's out, no more sex from me at all." And with those word's I took my supply's, loaded them on to the City van that I was driving that day and went about my job of cleaning the restroom's in different park's throughout the city.

With the number of men that I have been with, really each and every one of them, I figured that maybe I would be able to have a relationship with the men I've been with, like a long term thing, and that's why I gave in to them. Most never worked out and the relationship's I've had never worked out with a track record of no longer than a couple of year's, that's the longest any relationship has worked for me. I had never been to any sex orgy's, whenever

I have sex it has to be one on one, meaning just myself and one man. I don't get into all that other stuff, and have kept it that way. But I have gone through men like pair's of sock's, alway's changing them for another.

"Hello AngeLoner, AngeLoner!" Henry speak's out on the other end of the telephone. My thought's of thinking back to what happened between myself and Henry, and that I wasn't gonna give in to him again, had me in deep thinking.

"Are you finished with your work for the day? I know that you had to do Tom's work too. You did just dump trash today, right?"

"Yes, Henry I dumped all the trash today."

"I had to send Tom to another spot today because four people called in sick, and I was short on people today, but all four people said that they will be back in tomorrow. So we will have enough people to work next week, so you aren't scheduled to work next week, I am calling to let you know that."

"Yea, okay whatever, I won't be in next week then, bye." Oh, but if I gave into Henry's desire's, he would schedule me for everyday, but I wasn't about to give in to Henry at all ever again. It's been nearly two year's now, and Henry hasn't given up on trying to get with me again, but he had cut alot of my hour's to work since then.

I got my bicycle out of the locker room, locked the office door, went into the women's locker room changed out of my green uniform and into some tight low waisted levi's and sleeveless low cut t-top, I knew by looking outside through the window's that it was a hot day outside, so I got comfortable. I made sure all the door's were locked since no other custodian's were around then walked my bike out to Broadway and rode to Lake Merrit. Stopped at a liquor store and bought a six-pack of beer. At the same time I made sure that I still had the ten one hundred dollar bill's I had tucked away in my levi pant's button-up pocket. I just kept the money on me in case I would come across a nice studio I could rent and I could just pay for it then and there, I wanted to move out of that spooky ol' mansion in the worst way. But still since I have eight day's off, I might as well party a little. I am by no mean's a cheap person, but every time I have people over that I hang out with, specially at this time and that same crowd, I am alway's the one who has the money to buy the alcohol, I'm alway's the one with the marijuanna. Unless I would be partying with a man, then the man I am with will usually buy the alcohol but then of course, expect something in return, like of course sex. You know try to get me drunk and then take advantage of me. Only I never just give in to sex with a man just because he bought a few drink's. It's alway's the younger men who are attracted to me, and I don't know why that is, maybe it's because I don't go to the right places where the kind of men would be that I would be interested in.

Riding my bicycle around Lake Merrit about three car's honked at me, I guess because of the way I was dressed, but I wasn't stopping for no one. Even one man pulled up along side of me and motioned with his hand to go over to his car. He wanted to pick me up, oh no, that wasn't happening with me, I turned away from his honk I just kept riding my bike, and stopped at a liqour store and bought a six-pack of beer.

CHAPTER FOUR

LOCO

Good, I could see my favorite spot there at Lake Jewel under the lepta sperma tree, the bench there is unoccupied, and no one was around that little inset of Lake Merrit, I had the spot to myself, beside's one need's a City issued key to the lock on the gate to get into that area. I entered, sat down and I sucked down a six-pack of beer, had a couple of smokes and relaxed while looking at the beautiful view of the beautiful Jewel of Oakland, California, Lake Merrit.

I walked my bicycle back to the gate and used my City key to unlock it, took my bicycle back through there and locked the gate back up, then rode back to the spooky 'ol mansion. I had some packing to do, since I was finially moving out of there. But on the way back I just had to pick up two more six-pack's of beer so I could get drunk. I just couldn't help it, I still have energy, I still want to party, even if it was all alone. Just as I got to the top of the stair's, lugging the two six-pack's of beer with me, my pager went off. I didn't recognize the call back number, and I just felt like drinking right now, listening to music and dancing. The dancing is a real good source of burning off energy and burning off calories, so I could keep my flat six pack ab's. Let's see twelve beer's should get me to feeling pretty good, plus the extra six pack I had put away in the closet. My refrigerator was too small to fit three six pack's in it and since the two six pack's I just bought were still cold, I looked into the closet for the six-pack I had put in there earlier, what! It was gone, damn, someone came into my room and drank it when I was at work, yes they actually left the can's behind too, didn't even try to hide the fact that they were here. But who was here, I didn't know. Mother fucker's, like I wouldn't know that I hadn't drank them or something. Someday, whoever is doing this to me is gonna get caught, I just don't know who it is doing this, damn thieve's! I wanted to catch who was entering my room in the worst way. Burt was stupid enough to steal from me, and Oscar saw him coming out of my room, well I figured that one out.

Oh well, I just can't sit in this crummy place I called home and think about all the negative shit. I snapped a beer open and gulped it down, it sure taste's good and cold, especially after work, a cold beer alway's taste's good. I took off my levi's and top, and slipped into some sexy low cut short's and a white tank top. Then turned up the music, and moved to the beat, I love to dance, even if it is by myself. After the first fast beat song, I got out my marijuanna, and stuffed my pipe with some real green weed called 'white widow' took a few toke's, sipped on my beer, and danced to the next tune. The only thing I liked about the old spooky mansion is the big window and the view mostly of the sky and some house top's, with a small view of the bay. All I had to do is jam up my music real loud and if Burt is around he would soon be pounding on my door to low the music. So I jammed it up loud, drinking, smoking weed and dancing all into the evening is actually fun, I enjoy it and the excercise of dancing is great. No one came by that evening, I partied all alone until I just passed out sitting in the chair, I guess it's fun, simply because I can. I wasn't about to lay on the bed again after I found what Alix did to the bed sheet's when I was away. I've got to get back to that biotch about that too. If she doesn't pay up my hundred dollar's then I'm gonna have to kick her ass, lousey biotch!

The morning sunlight streaked across the room and shined right on to my eye's, as it had woke me up. The wooden chair was still proped up against the door knob, no one had come in while I slept, it actually worked, even the window latches were still locked. Although still weary about the opening on the ceiling, I got my flashlight and shine it up through the square hatch hole in the ceiling to be sure that there was no camera up there. I could alway's hear pidgeon's in the roof, but I never saw any pidgeon's up in the roof attic, but I could see the pidgeon's perching on the ledge of the outside of the building where the glassless window is that they fly into and roost, or whatever them bird's do up there. The attic must have alot of pidgeon crap up there since that is basically where the pidgeon's live and raise their baby chick's. And that bird shit would most likely bring rat's, yike's! But I had never seen a rat there, only snake's. But still, what weird noise's that pidgeon's make, and I mean some weird noise's! If someone heard those noise's and they didn't know that they were pidgeon's, thcy would probably be frightened to hear it, sometime's I had wondered about those sound's anyway.

With a slight hang over, I kicked back and turned on my small color television, and just thought that I would watch something on it for awhile, after all I have this week off of work. This time I decided to cover up the hole in the ceiling good with a piece of plastic I found on a desk out in the hallway. It looked like it came from a picture frame and was used in a picture frame. Well what ever, I spray painted it red got some nail's and my hammer and nailed the now red, plastic cover over the hatch hole in the ceiling, then I kicked back to watch some t.v. I had just hooked up a cord that came out of the wall to my portable t.v. set, plugged it in and it actually worked. For all that time I had been living in the 'ol mansion, I had never tried to hook it up before, but anyway it work's now.

There was actually cable here at the 'ol mansion and seem's that every station worked, even the premium station's with the hard core porn flick's. I don't watch porn, I would rather be doing it with a man one-on-one. But I couldn't help but to stop at one porn station when I saw a man with a real big, well you know what! He has black long hair, um I love dark haired men, only he is a little over weight, ah let's see look's like a little over weight and then some. But ummmmm, wow his thing sure make's up for that, wow! Oh, it is a documentary about this man's life of doing porn movie's, one thousand seven hundred and fifty movie's, he sure has been with alot of women, since I heard him say that he isn't gay, I assumed all women. This is his life story, ha, what a player. Well at least he get's paid for doing it, I think his movie's are more like a art to him, what a star.

No, I had no space to put him down after all I have been a player myself for many year's, and have been with at least two thousand different men in my sexual past. Being such a 'playgirl' myself was mostly because I alway's meet men here and there, like when I go place's by myself or even with friend that I sometime's hang out with I alway's end up meeting a man who will ask me out, ask me for my telephone number or give me their number. I had been partying since I divorced my first husband nearly twenty year's ago, and those year's all add up, alot of men that I have messed around with and had relationship's with throughout the year's, yea they add up. I slowed down with the messing around when people started getting Aid's, because I sure don't want to get it, I have been lucky not to have contracted anthing like that.

Except once I had gotten 'crab's.' That was a few year's ago, one day I just found myself scratching on my private spot and when I looked real good under a bright lamp and looked under my pubic hair's, there they were, tiny, tiny crab's. Oh no, I freaked out and went straight to the hospital and the doctor prescribed me some over-the-counter medication. It was a liquid that I had to rub on to the pubic hair's then comb it through with the small toothed comb provided with the liquid. But that was the only time I contracted anything sexual like that. I made sure they hadn't gotten on any other part of my body. Those micro crab's like warm area's to nest and cling on to, I got rid of those with the over-the-counter medication, icky!

My sexual affair's are alway's from trying to find the right man for myself, and I had never cared that if I have a love at the time, and another one come's along I check him out, but in no way can they hang around together, and I don't steal any of the women's men I know either. I have known many women that I've hung out with that has flirted with my man and screwed around with them, when I found out I drop them just like that. Although I must have had men that were true to me, I mean they couldn't all have done me wrong with each passing relationship. Any which way none has ever lasted, with the longest realtionship's that I have had lasted for a maximum about seven year's. To each his own, I've talked with a few women I know and a couple of them say that they never want a serious relationship ever again, and I believe them as one is in her thirty's and the other in her fourty's, they have experienced bad luck with their affair's and don't ever want to experience it again, I can't blame them at all. But they sure like going to the night club's and messing around with different men. But what will happen if maybe someday they find a man that they really fall for and want to keep, then they can't get serious about the man because of some different kind of a life's situation that they may be in. If in the beginning all those women want to do is have sex with the men, then they don't know much about the man and find out the very man they really like isn't availble to them. Then that is how feeling's get hurt, it is no fun to be in love and not be able to hold and love the person you've fallen for. Anyway, we change men like people change their sock's, if they wear them, get my drift? So even though I let those biotches hang out with me sometime, I don't hang-out with them often, because it can become a drag especially when some of the biotches that I know like to hang out at my pad for two day's at a time. Who want's company to come over and just hang out with you and drink your alcohol, smoke your weed, eat your food right from your rrefrigerator, even your last tv dinner, and use your shower and all that. Plus not kick down one cent to help you out with the cost of doing these thing's. Eating food, drinking alcohol, smoking weed, the use of electricity and water all cost money and some of my so called friend's like to do all these thing's at my place for free and not help with any of the cost's. I would feel like they were just using me to have a good time, and actually that is what they were doing because they knew that if they come to my home they could kick it, have a good time getting high, eating food, listen to music or watch a movie, spend the night, take a shower the next day like long hot shower's and not put out a thin dime, but have me cover it all. But just one day when I checked out my jewelry box, cupboard's, refrigerator and found they stole my pearl & diamond ring, then that same day my electric bill came in and was sky high, well that did it for me and I never let them hang out anymore. I didn't care if they even offered to buy the alcohol, I didn't want them around anymore, and I became a "Loner" and not hanging out with any of that crowd anymore. I mean after me being so nice and kind to them they treat me like this and steal from me, no, that was it for me. So if I hang out with any of them I just meet them somewhere else, but I still had to alway's come up with the high for a certain few of the women that hung out with me, they called me friend, but to me they were acquaintances and that's it. We would just hang out and party, sing, dance, drink, smoke weed, that's it. They are loud, never have money and can never ever find a man. It's like all the men they meet it would be a one night stand every time, worst than me and my relationship's. And the men they would meet weren't worth even dating anyway, they were as broke as the biotche's were and had less than them, but only wanted to hang out. One day the biotche's had the nerve to knock on my door without calling first, and they were with a couple of guy's that looked worst than Pegleg, at least Pegleg kept his clothes clean, but the guy's they were with looked dirty and nasty. I looked through my front window at them and told the biotche's that I was just about to leave, and that was it, I came away from the window. They knocked about ten more minute's, but I didn't answer to them, and then they finially went away.

And any man that I was with at the time, forget it, the biotche's eye's would stay glued to him and his body, and that is the way that they are! My homie's never have no money but depend on me to have everything to party with, the real only reason that I let them trip with me is because they themselves are a trip and my homie's. But I don't make it a habit hanging out with them, and it usually only happen's when I am in the mood to party, even once when they had taken the bart train to the most close station to my pad and called me up from the train station and ask me to go and pick them up right now, because they couldn't remember how to get to my place, just the Lake Merrit stop. I mean without them even asking first if I would be busy that day and ask first to come over no they don't even have the consideration to call first. But what the heck, they were my homie's.

Every time, and I mean every time that I meet a new man, after a few date's, I would only have sex with him believing that there was a possibility of having a meaningful relationship together, but time and time again the relationship's never lasted. I never asked anything of them. Yes, I have even had a couple of one timer's, meaning that I was with a man I just met for one night and that was it, never saw him again, that has happened to me a couple of time's in my life, I never made it a habit to have one night stand's with men, two time's was enough.

I turned my attention to the sunny view out of the big bay window's, as I watched a cute little black bird hopping across my window pane, I had noticed the cute little bird watching me through the window on several different day's. But I knew that if I opened the window to try to pet him that he would only fly away, and that's what the bird did as soon as I got up from where I was sitting and approached the window with some crumbled potato chip's to feed him. So I unlatched the window and left the crumb's on the window pane for the bird next time it came by to look inside, and left the window ajar, then here come's the bird again and peck's up the crumb's, he must have been very hungry because he pecked up all of the potato chip crumb's that I put out for him. Then I noticed that he tried to fly away and couldn't fly, that was because the little bird had eaten so many potato chip crumb's that he filled his little tummy up so much and he wouldn't be able to fly for awhile, and I sure didn't want him to fall so I opened the window more and his beady little red eye's look right at me, so I go to pick him up and he peck's on my hand, but it didn't hurt, anyway at that time I knew what was best for him, so I picked him up anyway and carried him inside. Snoop's look's at him and the crown fan on top of her head rises, but she doesn't screech out loud and that is a good sign. I set the bird on to the dresser that has a pencil holder that the bird perched on. Look's like I just made a new friend, the little bird start's chirping and tweeting, so I called him 'Twitter', I just let him perch there for awhile, singing away. Then Snoop's start's dancing in her cage and they were happy with their little visit together. After a couple of hour's Twitter could fly again, he flapped his wing's and flew back out of the window.

My pager went off, but I didn't know who it was because the call back phone number wasn't fimiliar to me, so I walked to the corner liquor store, bought

a six pack of cold beer and called the phone number
back from the phone booth.

"I lika to intraduce meself, I am Harry."

"Harry, I don't know any Harry."

"Yessa, you know Hajit?"

"Ohhhh, okay you are Hajit's friend, yea he told
me about you, how are you doing?"

"Oda, yedda, I fine! I lika cee you todey? Wherae
you livva?"

I gave him the direction's to get to the 'ol
mansion, and went back. When I got back there, I
knew there had been someone or something in my
room. After closing the door behind me I warned
whoever or whatever was there or had been there
that 'someday I will catch you, whoever is around
here, and I will destroy you.'

Harry showed up a half hour later, right away
we gave each other a big smile, as we had seen
each other around the station when Harry visited
with Hajit there. He has a thick black beard that
is grown just to his chest, he wear's a big turban,
the kind that can be unravelled. His clothes is the
average dress shirt and pant's. Harry has a nice
friendly face, and as soon as he shook my hand I
liked him, but mostly for a friend, I knew he was a
genuine man. Harry born in India.

But I could use a friend, and it was nice that
Harry was also only looking for a friend. He told
me that he has lived in the California for a couple
of year's and he work's as a Courier, and that he
is not married. He brought no beer with him but
instead a fifth of whiskey which led me to think that
he wanted a place to drink at with a person that he

could trust. Because Hajit knew me from work and know's I am a trusted person he must have passed that information on to Harry.

"You lika a drinka young ladie?"

"No, I don't drink hard alcohol much, only beer, but go ahead, I'll have this beer and turn on some music, do you like music?"

"Oh, yessa, veddy much!" He come's close to me and give's me a hug. "Oh, you ah smell veddy nice! But when I first camme into hedda I smella somathinga smella funny, what kind smella issa thata?"

"I don't know, but I smell it in this room sometime's, and I have the window open."

We forget about the smell after I spray the room with squirt's of my perfume. Then I started dancing, and that made his eye's pop out, he loved it and even joined in to his own beat of dance. We danced, talked and drank for a couple of hour's, he got smashed, more drunk than I did.

"AngeLoner, canna I ly back ona youra chair, I drinkie too much."

"Sure, go right ahead."

As he began to sit down he almost sat on a weird looking thing that I found in the closet when I moved into the room, I didn't know what it was it had sharp point's to it, and I thought that maybe it was some kind of a tool or something. I had left it on the chair earlier when I was looking at it.

"Be careful Harry, don't sit on that thing."

He pick's it up, "Whet isa it?"

"I don't know, maybe some kind of a tool?"

"I neva seen no tool like thet?" So he set it on the floor and sat in the chair and as soon as his head hit the cushion on the chair he passed out and just sat back with his feet up, out cold. I felt a bit sorry for him passed out there, he looked so tired, I just let him sleep.

I noticed the eucalyptus leaves had been swept away by someone, but who? I sure had no maid service.

With the music as loud as I had it blasting, I figured that Burt wasn't home or he would have been pounding on my door by now to tell me to low the music. Just then I pulled off the quilt that I had on my bed to cover Harry up while he slept so he wouldn't get cold. Then I noticed a big lump in the mattress, then I thought of how many time's I had felt a lump in the mattress as I slept there. I never really thought much about. Then examining it closer I saw a hole in it, "AHA!" There is a eye looking out at me, some kind of an eye staring at me through the hole. "Aha, I caught you!" I look over to Harry, he is still passed out, but I say to him anyway, "Look Harry, there's something in my mattress!" Harry doesn't respond to me, only with his little sleeping snore's.

"Aha, you sneaky thing, whatever you are in there." I got closer and looked into the hole in the mattress closely, yep that's an eye! It look's back at me and say's nothing, not a sound. I didn't want to get any closer to whatever was in the mattress, but I felt the evilness of it, whatever it is, without anything covering it up, it had a funny smell to it. What it is, I just don't know, it look's like some sort of an eye, and I can't explain it because it wasn't a human eye, but it was an eye. Then right at that time I got a call on my pager, as I looked at the number's that appeared on my pager, something happened to me, as if by reading the number's on the pager display I was put under some kind of a hypnotic mode. It was 'the man' who put that display on the pager screen, and part of my 'mission.' That is all that registered in my mind, that is all I understood and knew.

The situation that I was in right then at that time of something being in my mattress wasn't purely by mistake or wouldn't have happened to just anybody. I was chosen to do something, thinking that I had Harry as a witness to it. I soon found out he would be of no help to me, he was still stoned cold passed out from the whiskey he drank.

The number's that read across the screen, I remember reading them, but untill this day I can't remember exactly what they were, but by reading those number's it had put me into the mode to destroy whatever kind of a creature was in my mattress, only seeing it's eye. I knew that it was some kind of an 'evil alien' and not of this world. I jumped as Harry babbled something from his lip's in his deep sleep, then he started snoring real loud too. I wasn't gonna wake him up for this, the pager told me what I had to do, and that was to rid this world of the evil 'alien creature' that was in my mattress. I looked around the room to see what I could use to destroy this thing, then I saw the weird looking tool that I had found. I studied it for week's, then put it on the chair in the corner that I hardly sit on, then Harry almost sat on, I picked it up, and now knew that it is some kind of a weapon that I must use to rid this world of this, this, whatever it is hiding in my mattress.

Oh, but ugh, all those time's that I had layed there on top of the bed, on top of that mattress, that thing must have been in there, and this is why there were bulge's that I felt in the mattress as I layed on top of it to sleep on, I had even noticed a stinky smell coming from it. Good thing that I had never slept under the bedspread and on top of it instead. So the bulge's that I had felt while laying on top of the mattress came from that thing, whatever it is that is inside of my mattress. This was all so paranormal, no one would ever believe me about this, and although Harry was here, it's better that he doesn't know anyway, and better that he stay's passed out. But when I knew that this was all happening I couldn't help it but to say out loud; "Aha, you sneaky thing, whatever you are in there, I see your eye, I told you I would catch you someday, and warned you to stop hiding in my place, now I'm gonna destroy you!"

Did this thing, this 'alien', could it somehow or another come and go with the aid of someone? I had noticed sometime's the room smelled bad and sometime's it didn't. The foul smelling odor had been coming from that thing in the mattress, I know this because the closer you get to it the stronger the foul smell coming from it whenever I changed the sheet's, the sheet's and bedspread cover masked the smell.

Harry is laying back in the chair, sleeping cold out, with his head leaning back and his mouth wide open, he roll's over to his side, cuddle's up with his hand's in a prayer position, using them as a pillow under his head. Laying down sideway's now in a fetal position, he's still sleeping. My pager goes off, it had fell on to the floor off of the desk because it was on the vibration mode and it just jumbled on to the floor. I pick it up and there are a line of number's on it, I could read it well, after all I had studied the two full page's of number's for the accountant job that I had put in an application for. I'm real good with number's.

How is it that everything fell into place like this, when I had tried for the accountant job and faxed them from the unemployment office, they had faxed me back a phone number to call after I studied the two page's of number's to take an exam for the job, I actually had enjoyed doing accounting when I learned it in college, and I want a job that has medical coverage and some kind of a retirement so I could buy land by the ocean. So I studied the two page's with number's on it for awhile. But then after I had studied the two page's full of number's for all that time and I called the phone number that they had given me to call back and set up a date to take the written exam for the job, well the phone number was bogus. Then mysteriously the two page's were no where to be found when I looked for them again the next day. And that's how I learned to read the number's, but I never ever thought that it would make me a genius at reading the number's sent to me on my pager. It just come's to you and when you look at the number's it's just like reading word's. So many question's came into my mind, I had so many of them to ask, but who would I ask, who? Why was I chosen to do this mission? Who exactly sent me to do it? What would my next mission be? Harry was still passed out to the world, I let him sleep.

Then I moved the mattress around on to the floor, it was heavy and hard to maneuver. I pulled the mattress to the middle of the room, then it fell flat on to the floor, it made a loud booming sound when it hit the floor, flat. At that moment Harry threw his hand's up, then back down, and just went on snoring. I walked over to Harry and looked at him to see if he really was still sleeping. 'Huh, he didn't look like he was really sleeping, "Harry, Harry," I nudged on him, "are you awake?" I asked him as I waved my hand's in front of his eye's, still no response from him, only snoring.

'No, no, he is not asleep.' I could hear the word's of the 'alien' in my mind, but I wouldn't talk back to it, it was probably trying to get me off guard to answer it, that is what it wanted. But something kept telling me not to communicate with it, but why was it on this planet to harm many innocent people, or help, I just didn't know why. Somehow I just knew my mission is to rid this planet of it. I looked into the eye that was looking out at me. Had someone hurt whatever that thing is? I felt sorry for it whatever it is. When I moved the mattress I noticed what looked like green blood seeping into the inside of the mattress, I can see it through the pattern's of the mattress, and some of the green blood seep's through the hole from where the eye peer's out of. But this mattress is treated with some kind of plastic that stop's the green blood from spilling all on to the floor. I just somehow knew that the Space Alien was not gone yet, I wanted to spare it from suffering anymore. Then I realized I can't hurt it, I just can't, I jumped off the mattress I was standing on. This thing surely is not of this world, I've never heard of anything having green blood, what is it, where is it from, why was it bleeding green blood, and why was it bleeding at all, I never hurt it. I really didn't want to know, I didn't want to see the rest of what it look's like, there is a reason it is in my mattress, who put it there? Why me, oh, why me, why was I picked for this mission to do this dirty work of ridding the world of this, this, this thing? I decided that I wasn't going to do it, I've worked with animal's and the care of them all my life, I just couldn't harm it in anyway.

I could barely check under the mattress to see if the 'alien inside' would fall out of the mattress, it weigh's so much. Now I can see into the hole clearly as I squatted next to the mattress, the weird looking eye is looking back at me. What in the heck is this thing, the number's told me it is an alien. The alien wasn't make a noise, I have looked into many an animal's eye and close up too since I had worked around exotic animal's for many year's and I hadn't seen any eye that look's like this one. Then I look over to Harry, checking again and again if he is still passed out.

Harry still reclined on the chair let out some muffled fart's out as he snored away, he is still passed out from all that drinking, I couldn't help but to talk out to what ever that, that, that, thing was inside the mattress. Snoop's never made a noise, not a peep, she know's what's up.

"Whatever you are, I was told to destroy you! I've said over and over again if I catch anyone in here, and what ever you are, I will destroy, but I can't do it.

With an answer from it, I knew that the 'alien thing' was very intelligent, but for some reason it seem's to be powerless by being sewn into the mattress, or however it got into there. It spoke to me by telepathy.......

"No, no, no," I kept repeating, but I wouldn't concentrate at listening to it speak through our mind's, somehow I just knew that it would try to overcome me. How could this be, it's alive, it's here.

This is so real, yet so unreal at the same time, the pager vibrating madly, commanding me with the displayed number's to destroy the 'alien inside' of the mattress. The command's are real, I wonder who 'the man' is commanding me to do this horrid feat, but why me? There was no pay for it, but I know that it is for a good reason, all of these thought's fill my head. I could take this creature to a university or somewhere and get money for it, then when people can see for themselve's they will know that I am not lieing. No, I really know that wouldn't work out that way, I know I had to destroy this 'alien,' and that it isn't from this earth, and it is a very wicked being. But something else inside told me not to destroy this 'alien being', maybe all those year's of helping to train elephant's, and feeding and the care of all those animal's, both exotic and domestic. I knew that no matter what those darn number's on my pager was telling me, I wasn't going to destroy this, this, this thing. I had pity on it, but what would I do with it? What in the world would I do with it?

Then I looked straight into that 'aliens' eye and said "You must be destroyed. "Nooooooooo ooooo...................................." I walked over to the chair and sat down, I heard a gurgle sound., then I knew that someone had gotten to this 'alien' before I did, must be someone had harmed it and that's why it was bleeding the green blood. I thought of cutting open the mattress but I remembered what Oscar told me day's before, he actually told me not to cut open the mattress, because I had mentioned to him that I felt like there was something in my mattress. But how would he have known that I would have wanted to cut the mattress open, he even advised me to open the window if I take the mattress off of the bed, so I now opened the window wide. Looking down on the busy Harrison street below I had a decision to make.

I knew now it was hurting, I just knew this, as I felt a feeling of 'greatness,' that I had never felt before, a sort of a high feeling, like I had just taken something to make me feel good, real good. But I had not taken anything like that, and never had anyway, so like a natural high. I had just accomplished something by communicating with the 'alien', why this way, I didn't know, but something had to be done. This is for real, I thought 'what a feeling' I have at the moment, a feeling that I had never known of or felt before! I thought of many way's that I could have destroyed that 'alien,' but I couldn't do it, because I have a love for animals. even if this was a Alien of some sort. But this was not of this world, however I know it has a heart and it has feeling's. But what if it is wicked and bad, I just didn't know, and I just didn't want it on my mind that I had destroyed a 'alien'. It had actually made me feel real good, like I had done something good for this world, by saving the 'alien'. I just couldn't shake the feeling, the question, why me, why was I chosen to do this? Yet, I knew I wasn't about to get an answer, and no bother asking Harry. Snoop's must sense something.

I could hear someone pressing on cell phone button's, now where was that coming from, out in the hallway sounded like, but I peeped out the peep hole and saw no one, perhap's they were standing on the other side of the hallway. Then just at that time I could hear people cheering from the bottom floor of the building, coming from the main floor below. Alot of people were celebrating something, but what a time to hear cheering, just as the 'alien' was there, and I saved it from being destroyed. But that was for now, what was going to happen to it, I didn't know what to do. The sound's of people cheering and clapping was very loud, had they known that I had just spared the 'alien'? Was it all tied in together with some kind of a mysterious society? Or was it all a coinsodence that all happened with perfect timing?

Then there was it's green blood seeping from inside the mattress, WTF? Then again I heard what sounded like someone trying to make a phone call, like when the button's are hit on a cell phone. The sound was coming from right outside my room's door. I took out the small ball of paper that I use to cover up the front door peep hole so no one can see in and I looked out of the hallway, with only the dim light's shining from above the hallway, it wasn't bright enough to see all the way down the hallway.

Then Harry woke up with a loud snore and coughing, it awaken's him, he sit's up and look's around, feel's for his wallet, then he see's the mattress on the floor.

"Oh my goodniss, lady, what happen heare, why is thet mataress on the floora, and whatsa that green stuff?

"Harry, your finialy awake, good now you can help me to lean this mattress against the wall."

"Why youa put they mataress ona they floor? Ohhh, this mataress iz so veddy heavy, whaat, what iz thet green stuff coming out thet hole in it?"

"Harry, I don't know what it is?" I gave him some excuse that I was drinking some green soda the night before and it spilled on to there, only I don't drik green soda, beside's this stuff was too thick to be soda but that was an excuse to why I moved the mattress. "Come on now let's just get it leaned up against the closet, okay."

Ohhhh, this iz so veddy heavy, why is it so veddy heavy?"

"I don't know sweetie, let's just lean it here against the closet, thank's, right here will be fine."

"Ohh, it's a so veddy heavy and itz a stinky too!"

"Be careful, don't get any of that green stuff on you, well the mattress does have some kind of clear covering. Yea, sweetie it stink's so much, I don't want to use it anymore. Come on Harry baby, let's sit for a minute."

He then pull's out a pint of Wild Turkey 100% whiskey out of his inner coat pocket. And that was good because what I just went through, I needed a drink, and a strong drink too. After taking three big guzzle's, I tell Harry, "Thank's, I needed that!"

"But Hajit tella me that you donta drinky whiskey."

"Yea, well he's right, I don't usually drink whiskey, but I am now."

It was getting darker outside, we both heard more gurggling sound's coming from the mattress, it scarde Harry.

"Whet is thet noise, thisa place isa scary, let's go somewhere."

"Yea, okay, let's go!" I never thought that soon someone would be coming to take the 'alien creature' away. My mission was accomplished as far as I was concerned, I wasn't gonna destroy any creature. I had done what I felt was right. After all I am a regular person, nobody gave me a badge to destroy anything, forget those number's. I just left the 'alien' in the mattress, leaned up against the wall while Harry and I left.

"AngeLoner, whet iza thet happie sounz's of people clapping and cheerding?"

"That's 'cheering' Harry, and I don't know, it started a while ago, now let's go."

I opened the door slowly and looked down the hallway both way's, just hoping that Jack wouldn't show up at that time. We walked down the flight's of stair's to Harry's truck parked out in front, got into the truck and Harry smoked a ciggarette while we talked for a minute before he started up his truck.

"I need somemore whiskey." He hand's me a new pint that was in his glove compartmenty, he cracked it open and I guzzled some down. "Whew, ou wow that's strong, I'm high now!"

"Oh, I finish it, let'z go, I buy some mora!"

We drove to the liquor store, and parked by Lake Merritt for about an hour, it is only minute's away from the 'ol mansion, but I reminded Harry not to drink to much whiskey because he still had to drive back. Just then I got a page, I knew by the number that it was Jack calling. I asked Harry to drive to the phone booth just by the hamburger stand. He drove me right to there, what a nice guy he is, I needed a friend at that time, and he was there for me.

I called Jack, he sounded concerned about me and said he tried paging me earlier but it gave him a message that the pager wasn't in range at the time. But how would I be able to ever explain to him what had just happened, I just had no explanation for him. And how was it that your pager wouldn't have been in range, I was right there in the vicinity.

"AngeLoner, I don't want you staying at that mansion alone tonight, I don't want you staying there ever again darling, I'm coming over there in about an hour, please honey wait for me out front, that place is very weird, I'm so worried about you."

"Okay Jack, I will be sitting out front."

"Yea honey, just sit on the stair's and wait for me, and be careful sweetheart."

"Okay luv, I'll be careful, see you then."

I came back to the truck where Harry was waiting for me and as soon as I opened the door he tell's me that he got a page on his pager and that he had to go home. He live's with his brother and sister-in-law and they needed a ride to their Cousin's house. I gave him the tall cup of hot coffee from the store. That was good timing to, since I didn't have to explain anything to Harry that made it easier for me. We gave each other a big hug, and I made sure that it would be cool for Harry to drive since he hadn't drank anymore whiskey, he was fine, all the hot coffee did him good..

Harry drive's me back to the building. "Good-bye my friend, for now," he tell's me. I wave him off as he drive's away down the street.

I sat in front of the 'ol mansion for what seemed like hour's when it was only about one hour, then here come's Jack, he's driving his 1949 black on black Mercury lowrider. As soon as I see him I run to the car and when he get's out I rush into his arm's and I am shivering a bit because it is cold outside, plus what I just went through.

"Angel, are you okay, honey your shivering, get in the car for awhile so I can put my car heater on and warm you up."

He hold's me tight and can sense that something has happened.

"OK Angel, what has happened, I can feel it something has happened, what is it?"

I couldn't help it, I had to tell somebody, not even Harry knew since he was passed out at the time, so I told Jack the whole thing, everything that had just happened, even that Harry came over. I assured him that Harry and I are just friend's.

"Honey, we have to go up there now to see what has happened, are you ready?"

"Yes Jack, I'm ready, let's go."

We went up the stair's in the dark, all the light's in the building were out, even the hallway light's and the light's in my room. Jack had his pocket flash light on him, that lit up the room for us to see. He shined the light on to the mattress, "What's that green stuff on the mattress?"

"Don't touch it Jack, that's the green blood that oozed from that 'alien creature,' but now it look's like it has dried up to almost nothing and only stain's are left behind.

"I can't see much, it's pitch black in here, even the light's on the street are off now." All the power was off in the entire building and surrounding street light's, we didn't know how big was the perimeter of light's that is out.

At this point I didn't know what to expect, as Jack and I held on to each other. I need to get my coat out of the closet, help me move the mattress away from the closet door so that I can get it please. It's real heavy, so on the count of three we can push it away together. One, two, three..." the mattress flew up as we lifted it thinking that it would be very heavy.

"Angel, I thought that you said this mattress is heavy, it's as light as a feather."

Now that's a good question, it was just so heavy and now it is so light. Thinking of when it took both Harry and I to lift the mattress earlier.

"Yea, I know but honey before when Harry and I moved it to here, it was real heavy, I don't know what happened." It seem's that now whatever was inside of the mattress was now gone, but what happened to the 'alien inside'? But then it would be gone, and this is plenty proof that there was an alien in there, because the mattress being so light in weight now, and the green blood left behind, the smell was finially mostly gone too. Inspecting the mattress to see if it was the same one, I could tell that it is the same mattress, with the same peep hole and even the green stain's were still there, but no longer wet or drippy, but sort of dried up and stained now.

I had noticed early that day when I had looked around the room to see if I could find anything else that is strange or placed into my room, like when I wasn't there, I knew that people entered my room anyway. Under the edge's of the rug were like clear tube's with different colored wire's that ran all together and into a cut hole at the bottom of the wall's, but where it went to from there I didn't know. And under the bed itself, under the rug was a small white half dome shaped object. I discovered all of this when I checked out the room after I really realized that something isn't right here. I told Jack all about it, then we checked under the rug, and felt for the small half dome that was up under the rug practacially in the middle of the room, and under the bed, all of that stuff was now gone. I have no idea what the purpose of it was, and why it was there. But probably somehow it all must have tied in with the 'alien creature' being there.

"Angel, let's get out of here, we can come back in the morning when there will be much better lighting."

"But what about Snoop's honey, I'm worried about her being here alone now."

"If no one has hurt her by now they probably won't hurt her at all. But bring her with us anyway."

"Okay honey, let's go." I grabbed my coat from inside the closet as Jack got a grasp of Snoop's cage with the bird inside, we exited and locked the door behind us.

CHAPTER FIVE

"AngeLoner and Jack together"

As soon as I got into Jack's lowrider Mercury, he ask's me, "Darling, I want you to come home with me, please honey, you know I've fallen for you, I love you and I don't want anything to happen to you. It is your decision if we sleep in the same bed because if you want to you can stay in an extra bedroom that I have upstair's next to mine. But I would much rather you sleep with me, I will leave the decision up to you, what ever you want to do, as long as you come and live with me for as long as you want."

"Thank-you Jack so much, I feel so much better now that I know that you really do care about me and me being safe. I never wanted to go back to that weird building at night time again, or really at all. And oh yea, I love sleeping next to you" There's no way I could ever resist Jack, 6'2" muscular, but not too muscular, but fit, nice complexion, thick black hair that he combed straight back, nice haircut, but then of course in his job he has to have a kept up hair cut. Sexy mustache, brown eye's, nice nose and lip's, Ummm, he had it all. And the sex was just wow, wow, Jack liked alot to have sex from behind, expecially that last night together, that dark, dark, dark night.

CHAPTER SIX

"Berkeley, California"

I never slept in that 'alien' building again, moved to Berkeley. I wonder if Jack was a part of all that, we soon drifted apart. I often rode my bike up that long stretch of street, up Dwight Way, right past Telegraph Avenue, and have a seat at my favorite bench there in the People's Park. Usually with a couple of six-pack's of beer with me and a radio to listen to music while I got high smoking some good MJ, it helped out alot, to get into the groove, dig it? Just listening to the tune's and singing to them is fun and a trip, sometime's people came over and tripped with me or sing too, as they would even have guitar's or harmonica's, then sometime's have a 'sing in.' That night I had been drinking, and I was real high, even riding my bike up Dwight Way hecka drunk, I had almost rode my bicycle right into a big delivery truck that day, when I had just turned off in time, and continued to ride on the sidewalk for my own safety. There's a spot there where the police can't see you from the street as they patrolled by, because it had soon gotten dark outside, and the Berkeley police won't let anyone sit in the park or even be in there after dark like people used to do back in the nineteen sixty's. I met Hopleg, and one legged guy I knew from the past, he had lost his leg while riding on his motorcycle. We sat out of sight behind some over grown bushes, we just kicked back in the dark with only the street light's showing, drank some beer and smoke the best green bud. I got so high, and told Hopleg I had to go home now, and asked him where he lived at. That is when he told me that he just live's on the street, and often would sleep in a door way or right on the sidewalk, with his pillow and blanket that he stashe's away into a bush or side's of house's during the day.

"What are you serious, you just sleep on the sidewalk on some day's?"

"Yea, like mostly all the time, sometime's heck I roll into the gutter on Telegraph, nobody bother's me or the other people there, except for when I can find someone, anyone who will help me and let me crash at their pad. Like my friend Loc, he alway's has street people crashing there, but he is particular at who he let's to crash there."

"Wait a minute, you know Loc? Wow, what a trip, so do I. But then alot of people know Loc, he is a pretty well known advocate for the use of marijuanna, but then I guess you know that, if you know him, then you know what I mean, he alway's be talking about marijuanna and how he and other people are fighting the court's for it's legal use with people that have different symptom's and pain. Marijuanna help's with alot of symptom's when some prescribed drug's won't give you the same affect's, of just plain feeling better."

"Yea, Loc is alway's talking about the fight's he has in court and about, well actually, legalizing it more than having to have a doctor's prescription and going to the cannibus club's to buy it. Which is good because this way alot of street's are cleaned up from people not having to go out into the street's to buy weed. Wouldn't it be nice if we could just go into like a tobacco shop and buy good high quality marijuanna and not worry about getting busted, you know just like we can go into a liquor store and buy beer or hard alcohol."

"I hear you, I smoke marijuanna but I don't drink hard alcohol, and I know that hard alcohol can get you way higher than green bud's can. I mean people get more fucked up by drinking hard alcohol than smoking a nice doobie. Say, don't you know they have a club in the City that you can buy MJ there and smoke it too, we need more of those. But then you need a doctor's prescription to do so".

Well yea, I knkow that I have a card, but I only know of one place in Oakland. And Loc did take me to one of the Club's in the city where they have a counter covered by clear glass that you can see the MJ and buy it then go downstair's and smoke it.

"Well with weed, you can remember what you did the night before with weed, even though it is true that there is short term memory lost, like misplacing your key's or something. But then with hard alcohol the next day you might not remember where you went, what you did, or who you hit the next day when you wake up fucked up or in jail or

141

maybe even worst, marijuanna should be legalized, but for adult's only. I didn't start smoking weed until I was eighteen."

"Really AngeLoner, heck I started to smoke weed when I was fourteen."

"No, that's too young to smoke the schniznet, I think eighteen is okay though. Say Dude, were you born in Cali, are you from this area?"

"I have family but they all live in Georgia, so I am a far way's from my home town. I travel alot and every year about this same time I come to Berkeley, mostly to trip with other homeless that I know that do the same thing. I had alot of money from when I got into a motorcycle accident and lost my left leg, from the knee down......."

"Are you okay?"

"Don't worry my friend, it was a few year's ago, I've gotten used to it by now, but now I am running out of money and I have to file for disability".

I rode my bicycle slowly while Hopleg started walking next to me, we walked straight down Dwight Way, it was already late at night, I was surprised that the police didn't jam us up as to what we were doing on the street's that late, but they just passed us by. The street's were isolated as we were the only one's around, it was so quiet with barely a car that passed us by that as we walked the kerplunk of his wooden leg hitting the pavement made a loud noise. He told me that he couldn't afford to buy a new leg and has had that same leg since he lost his real one.

I felt so sorry for him, I mean him being homeless with no job, and being disabled with no help from no one. But then he need's to help himself because it is a cold and lonely world out there, and most people don't care to get involved. I sure don't want to get involved with him.

"AngeLoner, hey that's a sweet name, I have never heard that name before. You see, all I do is get high, day and night, and I even drop acid sometime's, have you ever?."

"Oh, heck no, I have never taken acid and I never will, so don't even bother to ask me to do none of that stuff, and I mean that. A few friend's of mine year's ago dropped some of that and they all went on bad trip's, with one friend of mine telling me that she saw some of her doll's crying and a bunch of other weird thing's. No thank's I ain't tripping that way, keep that shit away from me."

"I don't have any now anyway, all I have today is some good greed bud, we can smoke this." He pull's a fat bag of weed out of his pocket and show's me his bag of tight green bud's.

"Hmmmm, this is a twist!"

"What AngeLoner, what's a twist?"

"That you a homeless person actually has some weed, when every time I party with some of my homie's that are not homeless, they never have anything, not a dime, not no weed, not even can they afford to buy alcohol, and I am alway's the one to supply them with a high."

"Yea, well I don't have a dime either and sell a few joint's here and there to get money to buy alcohol, or work on a friend of mine's motorcycle that he is restoring, it's an oldie. I eat breakfast at a church close to People's park and eat meal's at the park daily, you heard of 'meal's not bomb's,' I have had many a filling meal at the park, thank goodness for the people there."

"Yea, I've heard of that program as a matter of fact one day when I was tripping in the park and those people were there with the meal's they called me over and invited me to have a plate, I made me a plate that day they had a buffet set up and I had some killer b-b-q chicken with salad, baked potatoe and some lemonade, it tasted pretty good too, whoever run's that program with all that food are very kind people." We finially got to the Bart Station. "OK, this is where we say good-bye, so good-bye". And just like that I got on the Bart.

CHAPTER SEVEN

Thinking Back To Worst Day's

It happened during the time that I let Alfred live with me, that was a big mistake in the first place. Alfred turned out to be a real creep. Alfred and I had been drinking one evening, after running out of beer I walked to the corner store to get another 12-pack of beer and when I came back to the apartment Alfred wasn't there. I had a suspicion that he was messing around on me with the boitch that was sneaking around the apartment's and running to hide from me when I came home, I knew that Alfred was sneaking her into my apartment that Alfred and I lived in. Because of a reflection on the window across the driveway one day when I saw her, Sue is her name when I saw that reflection on the window of her coming out of my apartment as I waited for Alfred in the garage she followed him out of there I couldn't hardly believe my eye's, but it was for real. I found out that she is a scrungha that Alfred knew from across the bay and that she moved into the couple that managed the apartment complex and lived two door's down. I figured that is where he must have went to that night so when I got back from the store I went and knocked on their door. For no reason at all the manager, and those two people I mean the manager's, Ray and Collette were no kind of good manager's for the apartment building, they didn't do anything around there except act like they are somebody when they are just crap! I went over there and knocked on their front door, I knocked loud just the same way they do to me when they knock on my front door. Ray come's ouside and pushes me down three stair's, I fall back on to the paved driveway and he jump's on top of me, pin's me down and start's hitting me all around my face real hard. He had my arm's pinned to the ground, so I got a hold of one of his arm's with my mouth and bit him as hard as I could. That made him jump off of me real fast. It wasn't fair, I wasn't expecting that to happen to me for no reason at all and a man too. He knew I have a mean karate hit and I ran after him he ran into his apartment and locked the door. I turn around to walk away and then from behind me here come's Collette out of the door without me knowing it she jump's me from behind and she is a big fat woman. She pushes me down from behind I flip over and she sit's on top of me, htting me. My hand's are free so I grab a hold of her blond hair and I pull on it as gob's come out of her head, I then start scratching the biotch. She is so chicken shit she get's up and run's back into their apartment. I start pounding on their door to come outside and I will whip both of their asses. I was ready for any fight in those day's and well prepared, but didn't expect for anyone to jump me without any warning. They wouldn't come outside, I was so mad and didn't feel the pain of their beating's at least not yet. I went back into my apartment, Alfred was no where to be found, he ain't much of a man anyway, and I never should have helped him out in his life. So that is how he repay's me for helping him get out of the gutter's, huh.

CHAPTER EIGHT

"Thinking Back to A Nightmare Life With Alfred"

At that time in my life, everything about my relationship with Alfred was so screwed up, I wanted him out of my life for good. After all if he hadn't been messing around with that biotch two door's down that herself was living in hiding because she moved into there, and Alfred talked to the manager's to rent her that room. I found all of this out without him telling me, and I'm not going to explain it all how I found out about that Sue living in that room, and running to hide all the time, I don't know what her trip is only that she has got to be the weirdest biotch I ever knew of. Thinking back to when Alfred and I was first together I was recalling some of the first day's of when we were first together. I would score my weed from Alfred in the City through a co-worker that I knew, we would drive over to the City in my car, and Walter my co-worker would have me wait in my car while he went into Alfred's flat and bought the weed. Then one day he took me into there with him and that is when I first met Alfred. He never should have taken me into Alfred's place to meet him, that same night he gave me his telephone number, I called him a week later and we hooked up. We started drinking and smoking his bunk ass weed that night, I got higher on the alcohol than on his bunk ass weed. And he never told me that he smoked crack until after he got me hooked on liking to go to his place and get high. I never should have even wasted my time with a low life like him. He didn't even have a car, well he had a Corvair but one day before we hooked up, he smashed it up and left it on Fulton in the City where he just let them tow it away. And why not that damn biotch would drive my car all over the City to do his dirty work of selling his fricking drug's, and never told me where he was going and what he was doing. What a waste of five year's with that worthless jerk, read on and you will see what I mean, damn worthless bastard! The next day after drinking all night with Alfred we had went to sleep together just before the sun had risen. I had to get up and drive across the bay bridge to my job at the County hospital. I worked in the food service department at that time.

A streak of the sun streamed through the window and shined on my closed eye's, the light awakened me, "Good morning," Alfred say's to me as I awakened.

"What were you doing dude, watching me as I sleep?"

"Well, yea I was, you look so beautiful as you sleep, and even more when you awake, I just get jealous of you when you sleep so well."

I thought to myself, now who would feel that way about someone when they're sleeping. I should have known then that he is a weirdo.

I told him that I had to be getting off to work and I had to be there by noon time. Whereas he had nothing to do all day except sell dope or maybe his friend Gene would call and get him a paint job that last's for a couple of week's. The guy was nowhere in life, and that is where I should have left him nowhere in life. But instead as you read on you will see where I helped him out by getting him a descent job at a park, and he end's up screwing around there too, but hasn't been found out yet, because I found out that he is still there, the creep!

I got up went to the bathroom, he came in there just as I was naked, he got on his knee's and start's licking on me then pick's me up and take's me to the bed where we have sex for three hour's. Until I looked over to the alarm clock and notice what time it is, I told him that we have to climax like now, because I have to get to work. We get more worked up, climax together, I get out of his bed, which is just a mattress on the floor, what a loser he is, what was I doing with such a loser, must have been the sex. I took my morning shower and got dressed. Now Alfred knew that my color television had stopped working a few day's before.

"You can use my smaller TV set, and take it with you now."

Well, back in those day's I was alway's pretty broke, not much money I earned at my County job, just enough to pay the bill's and a bit left over, in other word's I wasn't able to afford a new TV set, and people didn't use computer's alot like they do now. I should have guessed then that Alfred knew what I was thinking and finding out that he is a crack fiend I had planned to leave him that day and never go back to his place again. But he used his street wise mind and thought of the TV that I could use. Now he know's that I am a honest person and that if I borrowed the TV, like he offered me that I would have to see him again. I had no money in the bank, and lived from pay check to pay check, so I could for sure use the TV. Instead of that asshole tellling me that I could have the TV, he tell's me that I could borrow it because my TV wasn't working, I was so naive that I fell for it and agreed to borrow the TV.

Then his telephone ring's, he has a short conversation then ask's me if I could drop him off at a paint job that his friend Rene had for him for the day.

"AngeLoner, can you give me a ride to help Rene paint a house today before you leave, I don't have a penny to my name and I have no way to get there, buy this way I will have enough to take you to dinner tonight."

Ha, I should have told him, you mean some money to buy your crack to smoke. But instead I told him yes I would give him a ride, and I hope that it isn't too far. He assure's me that it will be close and then got the address to where the paint job would be at.

What a liar he proved to be! I drove him to the paint job which was halfway up Mount Tamalpias and by the time I got to work I was a hour late. Hello! Why didn't I see then that he was a addicted crack addict liar, and didn't care about nobody but himself and his crack. He sure was in bad shape, what a waste of time with Alfred, what a user he is, and I know that some people just don't change he was one of those people, but then again I know some people do change. Not far, bull shit, half way up that big, big mountain. No, he doesn't give a damn about nothing anyway, and especially not about me making it to work on time, he probably wanted me to lose my job, he was making me late all the time, I just should have hung him up then and ended our relationship. I went through hell and high water with that worthless jerk!

"Damn dude, you said it wasn't far, this is halfway up the mountain, I'll never make it to work on time!" Pulling into the driveway of the home to be painted there was Gene he was setting up his ladder's to paint the home. Alfred gave me a peck on the lip's as we said good-bye. He made sure to tell me that he would see me this evening, he didn't ask to see me in the evening but he told me he would be seeing me this evening. How could I have been so dumb as to fall for the creep. I actually think that it had something to do with him hypnotizing me. A couple of evening's before that he took a big crystal ball that hung on a string and he held it in his hand as he rocked it back and forth and told me to watch the crystal, and I did as he said, my eye's followed it rocking to and fro' in the air as he whispered word's to me that I just couldn't remember after that, he had me under his spell. He had nothing in his life, and the only thing he did worth anything was to play his guitar and give guitar lesson's, he make's money on the side giving guitar lesson's. There was really nothing else good about him, well except the sex that was good between us, we had alway's had great sex together, I guess that is most of the reason that I let him be with me. Anyway, I dropped Alfred off and went to work.

After I parked my car in the parking lot at the hospital where I worked at, I got a blanket out of my trunk to cover up the tv that was in my back seat. The county hospital paid pretty good and has some great benefit's, my job was washing all the pot's, pan's and utensil's for the entire hospital, I liked my shift from twelve noon to eight thirty in the evening. But still, after driving Alfred halfway up Mount Tamalpias I was late to work again. I had to explain to my supervisor that I had to drive from my boyfriend's house in San Francisco and that's why I was late. He made a note of it, and I knew I would be paying for it later when he told me we would have to have a meeting about me being late all the time. That just goes to show you how a man can bring a woman down or visa versa in this life! But I wasn't going down with him, that biotch, he's about as low as one can get, yet at that time I hadn't realized it.

Since I started work at noon time, Monday thru Friday, five day's a week, then that meant I stayed awake all night into the wee hour's of the crack of dawn. Getting all keyed up all night long, drinking, singing, dancing, we just messed around all night, or even sometime's by myself. Those day's, for sure were party day's. Then sooner than I knew it the day's turned into week's, as the week's turned into month's, then the month's turned to year's. Even before I met Alfred and I went with Frankie, I partied nearly everyday if not everyday and night.

Life to me was a big party, even when I had tried to kick it and have a quiet day or evening to myself, I knew that 'he' was lurking somewhere inside the crack's of the apartment building in San Leandro where I had my apartment at. As a matter of fact I had lived in the same area for most of my life, but at this particular apartment was where the weirdness began. Actually the weirdness began when Alfred came into my life, not when I had first went into his life. And that would have been the first time I met him when I went with Pete to his flat in the city. That was his world, his place. Wasting so many day's commuting back and forth from the San Francisco to my home and to my job at the hospital.

It wasn't that easy to get the job at the hospital in the kitchen department. A friend of mine that work's at the County hospital in Oakland doing housekeeping there had told me about the job opening where I work at, so I checked it out, put in a application, because first I had to qualify for the position and have enough experience to work there. I have plenty of experience, the next step was a written test, it was held at a local high school, there was a competition of hundred's of people. I passed the exam, I was number three on the list, then all I had to do was have a oral interview with a panal of three people. They asked me various question's of my past experience's and reference's and even asked to see how I would pick something off of the floor. I learned how to bend with my knee's when I had worked at the United States Post Office. 'Bend with your knee's, and not with your back. Anywho, a few day's later the head of the kitchen department at the hospital in the County called me and offered me a part time job, which I declined. I had to have a full time position with benefit's, then in a week he called me back again and I made the appointment set up for us in his office. He offered me the full time job, and I was in like flint, had it made, made in the shade o'Grady! Now I got a darn good job, with full benefit's, medical, dental, retirement, and PERS. I planned to make a life of it there, and keep the job which offer's the great retirement, and I was working pretty good there, until freaking Alfred came along. He wasn't serious about life itself and want's a ride down easy street, even if it mean's being penniless and broke all the time. I know how he does thing's, he doesn't! Ha hahahahha, he's a joke anyway! Only the joke was on me, I helped him when he had no place to live, I let him live at my apartment in San Leandro when his landlady threw him out of this flat in the city because he didn't pay rent for four month's. Alfred actually started painting the place so that he could show her something when she showed up at his door asking for the rent money. Then she suggest's that he move in with me, his girlfriend, yea, just throw your garbage at me lady. He begged to live with me and I let him move in with me, what a mess, his life and he threw that on to me too. That biotch had boxes and boxes of his shit in there and loaded it all in to my front room at my apartment when he moved into my place, it was like he came and just took over, probably just he has at the park where I got him a job, and believe me I never would have gotten him that job if I would have realized what a scum ball he is, I regret helping him out and getting him that job, I would be so glad if he got fired from there, if they could just catch him at doing something, because he is alway's up to something shady, I didn't know that about him at the time really, I began to realize that he was evil, but didn't know that he is wicked too. The man is shady, and nothing can change that about him. I hope that he hasn't harmed or tried to kill anyone else like he tried to kill me. But then I was still under that spell that he had on me, until one day I broke his spell on me and for a change I threw it right back to him, all of it, he can have that kind of a life, but not in my world.

Before that scum ball moved in with me, getting home after work to a empty apartment was kind of nice. At home where I could just spoil myself was great! I had my dinner at work and when I got home, I just kicked back and watched the 'borrowed' tv from Alfred. Within an hour the phone rang, it was Fabian, an x-boyfriend that I had went with for five year's and had recently broke-up with just before meeting Alfred.

"Hell-o."

"Hi AngeLoner, how are you doing?"

"Fabian, how are you, and how did you get my new phone number?"

"I saw Beth, she gave me your number."

Beth is a chick that hung out with me sometime's, she often went to the same corner bar that Fabian would often go to cash his check's at.

"I don't know Fabian, you know you and I have already broke-up."

His voice sounded so sad over the phone, that I almost felt sorry for him. So I answered him "Okay."

Just as soon as I hung up the phone, it ring's; "Angel? Hi this is Alfred."

"Oh hi Alfred, what's up?"

"We are up, what you doing tonight? Are we gonna hook-up?"

"No, not tonight Alfred, I have a bunch of stuff I have to do." He wanted to see me every day, and I knew why because I'm the only goodness going on in his life. The man is a crack addict, a small time dealer, and broke all the time. I knew that he wouldn't be coming over tonight without me telling him yes because he had no car and he wouldn't get on to the bus and the BART to come all the way here, and what if I wasn't home he probably wouldn't even have enough money to get back to the city.

"Yea, I made some money today and I thought we could go out for dinner or something."

Ha, I thought to myself, something would be more like it. He never ask's me out to dinner unless I tell him I am too busy, then he ask's me as his last resort to get to be able to see me and have somewhere to party that evening. I was beginning to learn the way his mind think's, and it alway's added up. There has to be something in it for him, and not for me, unless I am too busy then he break's out the asking to dinner.

"No, I will be too busy, so maybe tomorrow night, beside's I got to work late today because of giving you a ride to your paint job, and I gotta make it early to work tomorrow to make up for that time. I'll give you a call tomorrow, or call me." Damn he sounded like he wanted to cry or something, astonishing that the man had any feeling's at all, beside's sexual feeling's for me.

I then took a shower, refreshed my make-up, smoothed on deep red lipstick, sprayed some 'Hawaiian Lei' perfume, very expensive and very sexy. I put on some tight fitting leather levi's and a black low cut, long sleeve blouse that has silver button's running down the back of it, with a pair of high heel black velvet shoe's, and some black gloves.

Sooner than I knew it there was Fabian at my front door. As soon as I opened the door he stretche's out his arm's to me and we give each other a big hug and kisses hello.

"How have you been Fabian and what happened to your hair?" I asked as he took off his Oakland A's baseball cap. He start's to explain right away with tear's in his eye's.

"AngeLoner, since we haven't been together I have been just about going crazy, because I miss you so much! The other night when I was with the boyz (he has alot of family, Cousin's and Nephew's and Uncle's that are actually younger than he is, as he is in his late twenty's) we all got so high snorting coke and drinking. Then early this morning after not sleeping all night, I looked into the bathroom mirror and decided to cut my hair, I was still drunk at the time. I snipped off too much of my hair in some spot's, don't tell me I looked at my haircut in the mirror already, and I know that it look's terrible."

"That's okay honey, it will grow back, but till then I would advise you to keep a cap on your head in public. Hey good thing your job let's you wear a hat. Why don't you stop doing that coke anyway, you know that it ain't no good for you."

"Yea, I know, I know, I gotta quit it someday, but the boyz have all I need to get high on and they just turn me on to it for free."

"Oh well, whatever, don't even worry about it anyway, who am I to talk anyway, I smoke my weed, wanna smoke a joint?"

"Okay! But I want to ask you first if you want to go out to dinner?"

"I would except I ate a big plate of spagetti for dinner about seven this evening at work right before I got off, but thank's anyway."

"Then I'll order a pizza, okay?"

"That's fine with me baby, go right ahead."

We smoked the joint, and began dancing away. Within a half hour Fabian's pizza was delivered, with two six-pack's of beer, he ate half of the large pizza. I was having fun just drinking the beer and dancing away, but I did get the munchies from the weed, so I ate a couple of slices.

The tight levi's fitting every curve of my trim body, Fabian couldn't take his eye's off of my ass, and soon joined in with more dancing. Our bodies swaying together, not missing a beat, then a slow song came on, he put his arm's around me and held me close to him, it brought back so many memorie's of the last five year's that we have been together, that is until I met Alfred. And that was like jumping from the frying pan into the fire, because Alfred is a bad man, only I didn't quite know it yet at that time.

How was I gonna tell Fabian that this would be out last time together, I had to tell him because it isn't fair to him if I went on seeing the both of them at the same time, without one not knowing about the other.

Dancing and partying into the wee hour's of the night, the time came for the love making, after all we had been together for a number of year's. I still can't figure out what I ever saw in Alfred, the sex with him wasn't better than the sex with Fabian, what was I doing messing with Alfred. I guess that maybe I had gotten tired of Fabian, I mean being with him for all that time, but not actually living together. Fabian and I tried living together for about five year's, off and on. Every time I really tried getting serious in life about our relationship then Fabian would go on one of his 'getting high' binges and treat me real bad. He would get so psyched out when the boyz would come over, they would start talking loud, talking smack, drinking snorting and listening to music talking about time's ago and some of the bad thing's they did, working themselve's up into a frenzi of madness with all the dope and alcohol. Then by the time they would leave, Fabian would be all keyed up and fight with me, the next day I would have a black eye. I couldn't go on like that, and that's to bad that he get's that way, it would only be when he was around the boyz, other than that he would be fine. The day after he would alway's ask for my forgiveness, and I would forgive him time and time again, I couldn't go through that anymore, I was tired of all the physical fight's, and it wouldn't change because he would be around the boyz, his family and friend's and they would get high and we would go through the viscious circle again and again, it wasn't gonna change. So I decided tonight would be the last time Fabian and I would ever be together, I would screw him one last time and that would be it between us, I wouldn't see him again.

The dancing and holding each other so close made both of us hot, then Fabian say's, "Let's go to the bedroom honey."

The bedroom was only step's away we walked to there still holding each other, we just couldn't resist each other. "Remember Fabian kick off your shoe's first." With the turn up of the light switch my bedroom come's to life with the sound of the water splashing down the five tier's of my water fall and the colored light's around it that lit up. The tiny fishes in the water started swimming about as if asking for some fish food, Fabian feed's them a tiny sprinkle of food.

My bedroom is like a dream bedroom I have the hook-up with a big screen television, a all around sound system with a CD, DVD and video player, great to just kick back in the bed or sitting on the love seat. The stereo has huge speaker's, a microphone to sing on or record a song, a record player with oldie 45's record's to play on it, and even space to dance in. There's a small refrigerator in the bedroom, to avoid walking to the kitchen for a cold one and even space enough for a table and two chair's. On the wall's is wall paper of a country side and wind blown cloud's with bird's and a pond. The rug is a persian deep white rug, and I kept it white, all shoe's must come off before entering my bedroom. The bedroom is huge and I kept it extra clean and very nice.

We sure weren't thinking of doing anymore dancing at that time, I left the bedroom door open we were the only one's in the apartment. Then we started to get busy and make love for the last time together, only Fabian didn't know that yet that it would be the last time, but I know he had a feeling about it. It had been a hot day but not for us that evening as I had the air-conditioner on full blast. Thing's would be heating up soon between us Fabian has alway's been real good in the bed. We were up on the second floor so I just kept the curtain's open on the big bay window that has a beautiful view of the city below as the apartment is down in a driveway, yet up on a hill.

The bedroom is much bigger than the front room, I kept most of my more expensive possession's in the bedroom mostly because of when people come over to visit me, I know that some of them are thieve's and would even steal from their own mother, so when I partied at my place I simply locked my bedroom door so no one would go into there, and when the next day come's I don't have to check and see if I still had all my stuff or not. Because of my past experience's of knowing people and how I had been ripped-off in the past well I had to take extra precaution's of who to trust and who not to trust, and mostly with the crowd that hung out it was like trust no one.

Yet still, I hadn't really learned quite yet who to trust since I let Alfred hang out with me and I was about to make a big mistake by dropping Fabian and going with Alfred, what a mistake to have been with Alfred, no good, low down Alfred. I got my mind off of Alfred and concentrated on Fabian and being with him for the last time.

There would be no sleep tonight, because when Fabian and I got started having sex we went on for hour's, that is what I miss about him and his loving way's, that is when he wasn't all high and psyched out. The sun would be rising in a couple of hour's and Fabian would have to leave, I didn't want to risk having Fabian there and Alfred showing up.

Fabian and I layed on the bed facing each other he tell's me; "I still love you Angel." There he said what I didn't want to hear, and knew for sure this would be the last night with him, because I don't want to hurt him anymore then he already is, I just can't go on with him like that. I avoided looking him straight into his eye's because I knew that I wouldn't be able to hide the truth from him that I am no longer in love with him, and I am not in love with anyone, for now. Although his hand's were steady I could feel his feeling's of regret going back to the way he had treated me when we were together in the past, all of those five year's together. He had hit me too many time's, after he got smashed on coke and alcohol, even though it was those two thing's that made him act violent, push on me and I would push back and we had alot of cat and dog fight's. It just all flashed back in my mind then while we had a short conversation as we layed there, but I didn't want to bring it up to him, he would realize sooner or later about how he treated me so damn bad. Even one time he had given me two black eye's and knocked out both of my contact lenses, I had to go to the eye doctor have him take a look at me and buy some more contact lenses. But Fabian alway's covered his track's and paid me back for the new contact's at that time. He even made me walk home that night four mile's away, my clothes were torn and I ditched everyone that passed me by on the street, I didn't want anyone to see me that way. If some of the people that hung out with me saw me that way the way I was that night and they found out that Fabian did that to me, boyfriend or not they would have kicked his ass real good. I only tried to keep the peace, but now all those year's of the way he mistreated me where coming back to hit him right between the eye's. And this is what he will get for hurting me and wasting my time all of those year's, they say pay back is a bitch, and his is that, I'm dropping him.

Morning time, "Do you want to take a shower Fabian?"

"Ok."

We got into the shower together, turned it on full blast and took a hot shower together a long one too, we stood in there for about twenty minutes. I had alway's enjoyed out shower's together. Fabian would lather my body with soap and wash me all over with soap. And I would sud's up his ball's real good, too bad he had to get mean when he get's high, I kept on thinking about that, but I still knew that it was over between us.

"Say baby we didn't get any sleep last night, I have to be to work in about an hour."

"Oh, you work today? I wanted to take you to breakfast, which would almost be lunch by now, do you know that we started screwing about four in the morning and now it is eleven already, time does fly when your having fun, doesnt' it?"

"Yes, sweetie it sure does."

"I have to make it to work on time, I've been late too many time's lately."

"Why is that you just live a minute away from your job."

"Ah, well, um I wake up late." I sure didn't want to tell him that I have been sleeping many night's over in San Francisco.

"Sweetheart can I call you this evening?"

"Sure baby, call me whenever." I wasn't gonna tell him, no that he couldn't call me, I knew now that I was gonna have to ditch him everyday now for a long time, I just couldn't tell him that we weren't gonna see each other anymore, so I would just have to ditch him for day's.

"Good bye," I threw him a kiss good-bye as he went out of the front door. 'Whew,' I got a sigh of relief after he left, I sure didn't want Alfred showing up unannounced. I watched out of the front window as Fabian drove away in his Cadillac. And almost as if for perfect timing my phone rang and it was Alfred. Now how can this be it is almost as if he know's when I leave and when I'm here, or when someone is here or not. 'No, he couldn't be,' I thought to myself 'he just couldn't be spying on me, or was he? I truly hope not, I sure don't want to be with no psycho, I've had enough with Fabian getting psyched out for so many year's. But little did I know then that Alfred would turn out to be a psycho, as I found out year's later, a crazy ass psycho.

"Hello."

"Hi AngeLoner, what are you up to, had a nice evening last night? I would have called you back but I got busy, some people came by and I scored some weed and made a lot of sale's last night, how about a nice dinner this evening?"

"Aeight babe, but how about if I drive over to the city and spend some time with you at your place, I have the rest of the week off, and I can be there this evening after eight, I just have to finish out the week at work today, but they are gonna let us leave early today because of the holiday. Only I have to come home and do some house cleaning here." Saying that and thinking to myself of the way Alfred's flat looked, all messy and dusty, I thought of how in the world can I be with this loser. I didn't know that he had hypnotized me, I knew he had that crystal on the string that he would swing back and forth in front of me while he asked me to watch it as it swung as he would do this every now and then but I didn't realize that the creep was hypnotizing me everytime, at first I thought that he was just kidding or playing a game, but it ended up that he wasn't playing.

Changing my mind about coming straight home after work, because maybe Fabian would be there waiting for me then what would I do. Instead I packed a backpack of clothes that would last me for a few day's while I kicked it at Alfred's, that way I could avoid seeing Fabian and having to explain to him why I wouldn't be with him anymore, he for sure doesn't know where Alfred live's, all the way in the City, so it would be cool to kick it there for a minute, yea and that way I can get away for a few day's.

"No, I'll just be there straight after work since I get off early today I can be there about nineish, how's that?"

"Oh, okay, do you still want to go out to dinner?"

"Yea, that's what you asked me right?" He sort of sounded like he already changed his mind about dinner, and maybe smoked it up on his damn crack.

"Okay, we can go to this nice Thai restaurant on Geary boulevard, okay sweetie?"

"Yea, that sound's just fine to me."

"Yea, I guess I will do some cleaning up today myself for when you come over this evening AngeLoner."

"Alfred, you should do some cleaning up anyway, your place was a mess last time I was there, don't you ever dust? As you can tell I dust my place, but I'm sorry hon, I'm not gonna do your house cleaning for you."

"That's okay, I need to talk to you about something tonight anyway."

"Okay, I gotta go, you made me late already once this week when I gave you that ride up Mount Tamalpias, that was a trip, why you made me go all that way anyway, never again I'll tell you that much." I knew I was gonna have to dodge Fabian for some time to come, after all now I have someone else to party with, damn I hope that he doesn't get all psyched out like Fabian did. Knowing to myself that way down deep inside I knew that Alfred would never change from the way that he is now, and that he and I would probably last for a few year's together then it would be over, he would never mount to anything, always's spending most of his little money, or any money that he got for that matter, on crack or cocaine. And once again I was right, looking into the future that is exactly what happened, we lasted for four year's together, but read on about the nightmare life Alfred put me through even after I helped him out many a time's and pulled him out of the gutter, he went right back to the gutter, even though he has held a good job that I got him at a park in Oakland, I know he is still up to no damn good. But back then. still not knowing Alfred's real color's after work I drove over to his flat in San Fran. Getting right past the toll booth's on the bridge I could see a traffic jam straight ahead, damn I got stuck on the bridge for two hour's, good thing that wasn't the time of the big earthquake. By the time I got to Alfred's, there he was standing on the corner in front of his flat on Fulton. I pulled up in a no parking zone and let down the passenger's side window.

"What's up, I got stuck in traffic on the bridge."

"Yea, I know I saw it on the TV, let me in."

"Are we going to dinner now, I'm famished after waiting on the bridge for so long."

"Oh yea, but drive me to the Mission district first I need to pick up a pound of weed first."

"What, but I'm hungry now." That was just the beginning of his excuses, I went hungry that night and had no dinner at all because by the time I drove him to where he was going to get his shit and he bought a six-pack of beer, and he did the driving from there, I started to get high. We got back to his place at almost ten in the evening, I wasn't hungry anymore. There were so many time's after that he would leave me sitting in the car waiting for him while he went into houses, and left me sitting outside in the car for long hour's. Untill this day I don't know how I went through all his bullshit, while he was in someone's house getting high he left me outside waiting. What a sucker I had been when I was with him and under his spell.

The first thing that Alfred did was hid his stash, get out his glass crack pipe, take some cocaine, break some off into a spoon, add a little baking soda and some water to it and then burn the mixture in the spoon until it got to a substance that he filled his glass pipe with and sucked on that glass pipe and he got higher and higher, acting weirder and looking more crazy with every minute of puffing on that glass pipe. Rolling his eye's away in his head, and being really disgusting to see him act the way that he did when smoking crack, he acted just like a fly, a fly that was sitting on a big pile of shit, as he sat there on his brown recliner chair all alone. Have you ever seen a fly sitting there, rubbing his hand's together and rolling them over it's head, well that is the way that Alfred act's like when smoking that damn crack. He doesn't walk anywhere, he sit's there getting high, and even sometime's he will stand up and hold on to the heater acting like he is flying through the air and if he let's go of the heater he will fall from the sky, weirder than heck he is.

But I didn't care less about him, I smoked my weed, drank my beer and danced away to the booming music. Then I just started missing Fabian, how in the heck had I gotten myself mixed up with this loser Alfred. Heck, I had ten different men's phone number's locked into my phone at home, why settle for this crazy ass weird-o?

I've played the game in the past, having a dozen boyfriend's at one time, just pressing one button to call one of the guy's if I wanted to go out to dinner, or another button for a guy that would bring over some alcohol, weed or whatever I wanted to do for the evening. And every man look's hella fine too, but here I am with this dang crack attick that can't handle the shit he smoke's.

The lady friend's that I know well none of them are exactly ladies, I mean when I turn my back to them they would steal from me or anybody for that matter in a quick minute. So I just called them acquaintances instead of friend's. But they were a blast to party with and hook up with some guy's, and just drink and dance. I don't get in to all that other crazy sex crap like orgy's, no not me! I have never been to an orgy and I have had many offer's to do so, but I am just not that way. Although I may be with one boyfriend during the day and another in the evening, I never made it a threesome, no not me. I hate thieve's and have been ripped off a few time's myself but could never prove who did it. Some of my lady acquaintances I know are stone drunk's, and they are alway's broke, never having a dime to their name. Twenty dollar's to them is a big deal, and if they can get that much in their hand's they run to the store or corner bar and buy a drink. That's some of the kind of people I know, what a shame, huh? Why couldn't I meet anyone of my caliber, no I just knew alot of drunk's. And when they came to visit me they would want to stay and party and get high for day's on end, and of course that would be to my expense, I would cover everything. Yea, once in a while they would have a dollar or two to throw into the pot to get high with but being me I would just tell them to keep their money, and I paid for all the alcohol and alway's kept the best marijuanna to smoke. Like Nannette, when I took her to places, and especially to a past boyfriend of mine's just to visit, heck I didn't want the guy no more so I let her have him. And every one of them would end up screwing Nannette and forgetting about her, except one of my exes, she and him were together for about two month's they lasted together until he had enough of her mooching off of him and he threw her out into the street's one night. I had to go and pick her up off of his front porch and take her back to her place where her husband Dale would be waiting for her at. But of course he didn't know about her way's, but he must of had his suspicion's. Then when Nannette's daughter made eighteen she started partying with her mom, they came out to my place in Berkeley and Nannette started drinking up all the tequila and she got stoned, then just layed on the couch and wouldn't get up and leave, I just wanted the both of them to leave my place. Until finially I figured it out a way to get her ass up, I took thirty dollar's out of my pocket, and told them, 'Here's this thirty buck's if you both just leave." Man, she got her ass up off of the couch so fast and she and her daughter were out the door in five minute's, promising to pay back the thirty dollar's on welfare check day. I told them 'oh yea, un huh, sure!" I knew that they would never pay me back, I just wanted them gone and they were, however that wasn't the last time I let Nannette hang out with me.

The last time we hung out together was one night when we ran out of gas and two young guy's saw us walking down the street to get to a phone booth, they pulled over and asked if we wanted a ride.

"No, we don't want no ride." I yelled over to the guy's.

Then Nannette scream's out, "Wait a minute, I want a ride!" Then they back up the car to talk to her. I told her don't go with them, you don't know them, beside's your gonna leave me alone on this dark street, because I ain't going with them.

Right away Nannette jump's into their car and one of the guy's that got out to let her into the car was telling me to get into their car and he tried to grab me. But I pushed him back and did my karate dance, he knew I would have whipped his ass if he touched me, that scarde him and he jumped back into the car, with Nannette sitting between the two in the front seat of the car.

Thank goodness that I made it safely back to my place that night, I had jogged back all the rest of the way alone, as I dodged every car light that came my way. I was very lucky that I didn't meet up with anyone that was walking my way and saw me alone, because who know's who will be out there at that time of the night. I would have hummed for Loco but I just wanted to hurry back to my place, beside's I had my three inch pocket knife on me that my mother gave to me year's before that I alway's carry on me.

The next morning I called up Nannette, mostly to be sure that she was okay, and asked her why did she go and leave me there walking on those dark street's alone even after I told her not to go with them.

Nannette tell's me, "I wanted to go with those guy's, beside's they gave me fifty buck's to suck them off."

"Ewwwww, ugh Nannette you are nasty, don't ever bother to call me again, I don't want you and your nasty self around me anymore, good-bye!" And that was it, we never hung out together again. She wasn't a player, she was just a hoe.

Getting back to that evening with Alfred, yea he got double stoned that night like every other night after that, he would smoke his crack pipe, and act like a fly. Dodging Fabian for awhile wasn't too easy, because I didn't want to go back to my place until I made it plain to him that him and I was over. I still can't grasp on to dropping one man for a worst one! But at that time I excepted Afred's smoking crack, and there's that night I tried smoking it, I swear it took me to the moon, I actually felt like I was walking on the moon, it's like this, you take a hit, inhale the smoke, hold it in, and then it take's over your mind and your body. Crack is the kind of drug that make's you instantly do shit that you would never ever do, if your a person with moral's and ethic's, well crack can change that for the worst, and if you smoke it, for sure it change's you to do stuff you wouldn't normally do. So if a type of person that don't give a shit what they do smoke's it, then that's right up their alley because they will do anything to get some more of it, and that is how controlling it can be, if you let it. You are not in control of smoking crack if you smoke it and like it, it is in control of you. I hated it, after that first trip, I knew that the drug is a very 'wicked' thing to do. I would advise to anyone not to do it, either you like 'crack' or you don't and if you do like it then your in trouble. Even if you have alot of money to buy 'crack' it doesn't matter, it is still a bad drug to get hooked on, even for one's health. But mostly because it can make you do thing's you normally would never do, imagine that, getting hooked on it and controlled by it's high, now that is scary! All I would say is don't do it, ever. And that was it for me, after that night, I never smoked it again, I did not like the high at all, nope not one bit.

Whereas unlike marijuanna, now that is different and a natural high, it is not processed but straight from the earth. It help's people that are in pain and prescribed to do so. It has a mellow high and make's you have quite an appetite after awhile. You may find yourself stuffing all kind's of food down your throat faster than you can eat. So smoking alot of weed sure can make one over eat. I smoke the best m.j. and even prescribed to do so, but even though I have cut down on smoking weed everyday, and now just smoke weed when I want to be mellow. Just plain herb from the ground of mother nature with no additive's, sound's fun to me! But I really believe that not smoking anything is the best thing to do, it is the choice of each of us individually.

Staying in the City with Alfred meant party time is 24-7, his flat is right across the street from Golden Gate Park, right across from the panhandle area of the park. It's a nice location and especially if you like park's, which I do. That next day we walked across the street to the park and had a picnic with some wine, sandwich's, potato salad and chip's. We sat by one of the the many, many small lake's that is in the park and watched the duck's diving into the water. Then we saw the strangest thing, latched on to a tall plant stem were two weird looking bug's, evidently a male and a female, the male had a big and long sex testicle and the two bug's were mating there on the stem and they were still going at it hour's later when we checked to look at them before our picnic was over. So you can see all kind's of different bug's and bird's and many beautiful colorful flower's, plant's and tree's growing in the park. That's a little something about the bird's and bee's for ya.

Day's passed by, I got tired of Alfred getting high on that whack crack! The next morning I awoke before he did, he was out cold from getting so high all night, he layed there still passed out. I got up off the mattress on the bedroom floor, put on my clothes, left a short note for him to find when he awakened, and got in my car drove back across the bay bridge and made it to work on time this time. It had been a long four day week-end with the two extra day's for the holiday's. I soon learned that holiday's were just another day to Alfred, and we did nothing nice for the extra two day's. I knew this yet I continued to see him, his only quality is being a con man, if you can call that a quality, it is a bad quality.

I went back to work that day and actually made it on time and that was because I didn't wake up at Alfred's house, as he alway's made me late to work. But when I got to work there was some new guy doing my job, and I was told to go to the office. We had a meeting, and were to have another meeting with a union representative next week, to see what was gonna happen to my position there because of me being late all the time. There was no use in arguing with them, I was told to go home until the meeting next week.

Well that sucked, now I had no job, and it was because of Alfred, he had no job at the time, except for helping his friend paint and selling drug's, other than that he had nothing going on for him. And now I didn't either really, he was slowly pulling me down to his level with him. But there was no way that I would ever, ever be like him. Beside's I knew that I was just suspended for those day's, and with the union rep there I would get my job back after the meeting next week.

So I went back home, and on my telephone was a message from Alfred it was; 'AngeLoner, I'm leaving you this message because I just called your job and was gonna leave a message to have you call me. I wanted to get in touch with you before you get off of work this evening, you left your pager here, but it's not working, I don't know why. Anyway I wanted to ask you if you want to go to a Giant's ball game tonight at the stick, call me back and let me know.'

I then checked my purse, yea my pager was missing, but I know why it doesn't work, I took the battery's out just in case Fabian paged me, and Alfred is too dumb to check that, beside's why should he check the battery's, he probably don't even have enough money to buy new battery's, and if he did he is so cheap he wouldn't buy them for me anyway, but go straight out and get his coke to cook and make him some crack. I don't know why, but I called Alfred right away, not thinking about it but actually now that I had all these day's off of work, I really wanted some quality time of my own, to kick it alone and just take it easy for awhile.

When I called Alfred and I told him about my job and what had happened, he had the damn nerve to tell me to be sure to make it to work on time next time. What an asshole, he know's that it is mostly his fault for me being late all the time, and if he was any kind of a descent man he would have tried to help me to make it to work on time. Really, I think that this is what he had planned so that I spent more time with him, the jerk!

I accepted the invitation to the ball game, and drove over to the city to Alfred's, the day went by quickly and in the evening he drove us in my car over to the ball park. On the way he gave me the new's that his landlady gave him thirty day's to move out, and he didn't know what he was gonna do with no where to live at and no money to get a placc to live at. Again, I fell for his sad story's and gave into his plead's and told him that he could come and live with me in my apartment. What a mistake to take him in, what a waste of the year's ahead with him, what a nightmare my life became with a no good man like that!

It was a good thing that when my daughter Terces got old enough she went off to college, good thing that she didn't have to live there and see how Alfred lived, just moving in on me.

After the game, the Giant's won, Alfred wanted to celebrate, hah, what a joke, he already celebrate's something 24-7 anyway, how was it supposed to be different tonight. It was late, the game was a double header and it was already past midnight, so we drove back across the bridge to my place. I never thought that Fabian would show up but he did just minute's after we got to my place. I hadn't even had any time to turn on some music, I was busy loading the refrigerator up with a 24-pack of beer. Shock, Alfred had enough money to buy it, plus he had a couple of joint's. He was already sitting at the couch smoking up a dove when a knock came to the front door. I peeked out the front window and there was Fabian standing there. Oh snap's, what was I gonna do now? Alfred was in a world of his own, he was so high that he hadn't realized there was a knock at the door, he sat there, high as heck doing his usual fly impression. I didn't answer the door, but I could see Fabian walk back down to his car parked in the driveway as he stood in front of it, sipping on bottled beer and looking up to the window. A few minute's went by, and Fabian honked his horn, it sounded real loud. Alfred came out of his daze and ask's me who is that honking outside. I told him that it is a guy that I know, so be quiet because I don't want him to know that I am home. But instead Alfred slide's the window open and stick's his head outside and yell's down to Fabian that I wasn't home, then shut's the window back, and sit's back down.

"I told you to be quiet, I didn't want him to know that anyone was here!" He did that on purpose.

Fabian was now hip to what was going on with Alfred and I, a beer bottle came crashing through the window and just missed Alfred's head. But chicken shit Alfred just sat there like a fly and paid no attention to it, but he knew what was going on too. Fabian reved up his car and sped off, leaving behind a cloud of dust and a long skid mark, I never ever saw him again after that, and of course, I never called him again either. But between the two of them, Fabian was the better man, if only he wouldn't get so mean when he got high. But then Alfred turned out to be worst.

CHAPTER NINE

"A Baby Boy Is Born"

It had been a year since Alfred and I broke-up, but I was still running, just in life itself, not running from no one, but I knew that I was being stalked by someone. I had taken a bike ride earlier that day and strangely I felt as if something fell in my stomach, so I went to lay in my bed. After breaking off with Alfred a year ago, thing's had changed. It would be the last night at the 'ol mansion, then I would live with Jack, whom by now I had been with for nearly a year. But then there was that one night we got together about nine month's ago. It was wonderful, the sex was so wonderful. I didn't have a cell phone in those day's, and even though I should have called Jack again, I never did. He got kind of pissed off at me once before that and told me not to call him or he would get me into trouble. So even though we got together that one night, nine month's before, I never called him back.

Falling into a slumber, and very deep sleep, even though my eye's were closed I could hear talking outside my bedroom door coming from the hallway.

181

I couldn't quite make out what the people were saying, it was a different woman's voice that I couldn't identify with. All I could make out is that I could hear a female unfamiliar voice talking to the man I rent the room from and telling her to get out of her bedroom, but she was refusing to do it. Then the room mate screamed, 'Ouch, you twisted my toe, oooouuuuuuuuch, that hurt's!' Then I could hear her crying, but I couldn't move, it was like I was sedated. What the heck was going on, I tried waking up but couldn't, yes someone had sedated me somehow. Was it something I drank, was it done in my sleep, after all my door could have been jimmied open at this place. Then I knew that the open liter of root beer in the refrigerator must have been spiked, darn something told me not to drink it, but I did, I drank a cup of it. I fell back into a deep sleep, awakening every now and then. And after what it seemed to be like an hour, I heard that woman's voice again, it was coming from inside of my room this time. She shook me a little, I opened my eye's, she told me to look at my new baby boy that was just born. I saw him a beautiful baby boy, "Ohhhhhhhhhhhh he is mine, oh, I love him, I will name him the same as his half brother, I want him, I want him, let me hold him."

But the strange woman laugh's wickedly and tell's me, "Yes, this is your newborn son, and you won't remember any of this, we're taking him."

"Please, don't do this, don't................" I plead to her not to take him away from me, "don't take him from me, pleeeeesssse, my baby, give me my baby, nooooooo, don't take him awayyyy............." then

I feel a small pinch on my arm and see the needle she just stuck into me, I fall back into the drugged sleep she put me in, I was helpless now that she had me sedated, I couldn't fight back for my newborn, he was abducted, kidnapped, taken away, and there was nothing that I could do about it.

Hour's passed by, the sun shine peeked through a cloud and streaked across the room on to my closed eye's, the brightness awakened me as I slowly opened my eye's, I sat up and shook my head, still feeling a bit dizzy from the spiked soda. That's what I remembered, I couldn't remember at that time about the shot. At first I didn't know if it was a hangover or not, but then I thought back. That woman was wrong, I remembered it all, my baby that was born and taken away from me, I remembered it all!

'Oh what a night last night was,' I think back rubbing on my forehead, I begin thinking back to what had happened. 'No, it couldn't have happened,' but it did happen. On the floor in one corner of the bedroom I noticed one of my bath towel's laying there, 'now that towel wasn't put there by me, I just don't leave towel's or clothes laying around.' I had my own hamper that I put soiled clothes or towel's into. I got up, and I could feel that I really had given birth, it was true! Menstrual blood ran down my leg's, I first got a clean towel and wiped myself off then got a kotex and put it on. I then picked up the towel off of the floor, and I can see a round shaped stain on the towel, the stain was still damp and I couldn't help but to remember the smell of it, the same scent like when my daughter was born, newborn's have a certain smell to them and childbirth, yes, that was the smell of the towel.

I got another fresh towel from the stacked clean one's in my closet, I had to take a shower, then got my bathroom basket, in it I keep all the item's I need when I go to the bathroom across the hallway to take my shower's. 'Oh, am I flowing heavy today, ow my stomach hurt's,' I had to sit back down for a minute from feeling ligh-headed. 'No, no, no, I thought, 'I gotta get up and take a shower,' I felt so bad when I realized my baby was taken away from me. I had a feeling I was pregnant, but it never showed that much and I just thought that I had gained weight, when all the time I was pregnant. I wanted my baby, I want him so bad, I miss him, I knew it, he is a part of me and alway's will be. So many thing's was going through my mind, where is he, will I get him back? Suddenly my newborn's face flashed in my memory, tear's fill my eye's as I think of the night before, I wanted my baby soooo bad, I want him back, where is he? All the question's filled my mind, I got my shower's necessity's together and opened my bedroom door, no one answered me as I called out if anyone was home. My roomate's door, the door was wide opened, I could see that no one was in there. I went into the bathroom and took a long hot shower, I knew it was true and that I had just given birth, I could tell the way that my body felt, it was the same feeling I had after the birth of my daughter. When I got out of the shower and crossed the hallway to my room, I called out again down the stair's if anyone was there, but no one answered.

In my room I opened up the curtain's to my second floor bedroom, the sky's blue, bird's singing, but I felt so tired, I closed the door and lay down on my bed and wept because my mother's instinct's told me that my baby was gone, taken away from me, kidnapped. I could remember the woman that held my newborn and something about her having a camera. I drifted off to sleep with tear's in my eye's, I slept thinking of flash back's of what I had just went through, I want my baby boy back, I missed having him close, I love him. How could this have happened, why hadn't I went to see a doctor when I had the feeling that I was pregnant. I should have known because I missed too many menstrual period's, but I just thought that it was because of the stress in my life at the time, but it wasn't because of that but because I was pregnant. What was I gonna do now, oh what was I gonna do to get my baby back? It was Jack's baby, I knew that, after being with Jack I was with no other man, nobody.

I wakened when I heard a door slam, so I got up a bit woozie and looked out my door to across the hallway where I could see someone was sitting on the bed, so I called out, 'whos's there?'

"It's me AngeLoner, Dale." I walked to her room, and there she sat up in her bed with her toe plastered up.

"How you doing? Hey, what happened to your toe?"

"Oh, I accidently bumped it, that's where I just came from the doctor's office, he fixed me up, I just have to stay off of my feet for now."

"Yea me too."

"Huh?"

"Oh, I have a flu or something and I don't feel too well, I'll probably just kick it here today."

"Fine, whatever."

I wasn't about to tell her what she must already know, she has to be in on knowing about my newborn, she just has to be, I just know it. Then I remembered yesterday when I was in my room and I overheard Dale screaming about someone hurting her toe, she hadn't bumped it after all, liar! From that day on I knew that I had to move out of there, but I still wanted to find my newborn. All morning I sat on the chair on the table, looking out of the window, up to the blue sky, watching the cloud's pass by, sometime's watching television or playing solitaire. Then it hit me again, Jack's baby, I still love my baby boy, I have to find him, I have to see him and hold him, I need my baby, I want him back. I knew the baby was not from Alfred, but from Jack.

It was then about lunch time, I got a can of soup out of my closet for lunch. After last night and feeling the way I do, until I move out of here I am not eating any thing that is already opened, I know that I was drugged. When I got down the stair's there was a man, and that woman, the woman that had that camera last night. Before I could say anything to them, the man tell's me that they are cleaning out the air duct's, and putting in a new washer and dryer. The woman look's at me like what was I doing walking down stair's. I dogged them both, meaning watched them carefully, at that time she had no camera but then she did something weird. I proceeded to make my canned soup, after all what was I gonna do, tell them off and question them about last night when I knew that they weren't gonna admit to anything, I think not. The woman walk's outside and return's with a camera, she didn't take any picture's but instead was holding the camera as if she was protecting it or something. That bitch made me lose my appetite, but I poured the soup into a cup, and went back upstair's without any of us speaking to each other again. I ate the soup down, got dressed, grabbed a pencil and paper, stuck that in my pant's pocket and went out the front door to get the license plate number to the white van that they were driving, I knew that it was there's because here come's the woman again with the camera in her hand, but I never let her see me getting the license plate number. On my way back in I saw a newspaper on the door step's, so I quickly picked it up and took out the 'for rent' section, I had decided that I was gonna move out of there as soon as I could. Making quite a few trip's to the bathroom because I was flowing so heavy, I had to take care of my personel hygiene. Then I went back down stair's and the couple was gone. I checked to see if they had put in the washer and dryer, I noticed a new washer but the same dryer was there.

I went back to my bedroom and put on the same blue jean's I wore yesterday, I noticed that now they were to big for me and how stretched out they had gotten, no wonder these were the only pair of jean's that I had fit into for the last few month's, I was pregnant. I took out another pair of levi's that I hadn't word in month's because they had gotten too tight to wear, but now they fitted me, they were a little tight but I could now fit into them, and that's telling me something.

Yesterday was my birthday, Oh my gosh, my baby boy was born on my birthday, October 5th, it was now 1994. October 5th, 1994 that would be his birthday. Strange how they wanted me to name him, I told them Paul like his half brother. Thing's like that would happen to me all the time, like one of my daughter's was born on Thanksgiving, the other on Labor Day. Now my newborn was born on my birthday, purely coinsodence, I don't think so, it is all true, and I know it. What was gonna happen with my newborn, were they gonna sell him, keep him, oh, where is he, the tear's streamed down my face, I cried and cried for him and had my music turned up loud so that no one could hear me cry. But anyway they know what's going on, I wanted a cold beer, I know that Roger, Dale's husband kept cold beer in the refrigerator in the garage and I had never touched that beer before, I never drank any of their beer before, but fuck it, the occasion called for a cold one, I headed downstair's to the garage. Passing Dale's bedroom first I could see that she was no longer sitting up in her bed, when I got downstair's I could see that there was no one there except me.

'Cool, I thought, I'm glad to be here alone today, but for how long will it be before someone get's back?' I guzzled down a couple of beer's and checked through the rental section of the newspaper.

I only want to have a little space of my own that is close to commute to work, a place that is safe to live at and enjoy myself whether alone or with some company, but can I find a place like that to rent, I searched the newspaper for a place to rent. I wanted Molly to live with me but she has her own place, it is alway's nice to have family live together, that is as long as you get along well, and Molly and I alway's have. But I couldn't tell her about her baby brother, at least not yet, not until I find him and hold him in my arm's once again, I miss him so, and love him so much. But that may never be that I tell her because I may never ever find him.

CHAPTER TEN

"The Mystifying Park"

Walking past the deep pond in the park area I notice a pair of eye's peeping above the water and a snout with the outline of a back and tail, I know there is alligator's in the water, after all I had taken care of alligator's for year's at the City zoo where I worked at. But why bother with them or telling animal control about them, they would have to drain the big natural pond to find that out, or sit by the pond for hour's on end to see if they could catch a glimpse of the 'gator's, and I know that they wouldn't be bothered about it. So I made sure that I kept a distance from the pond for my own safety. I know nobody swim's in there because the water isn't that clear at all, and you can't see very deep into it, but I figured somebody was feeding them.

I proceeded on to the restroom's that I had to clean. First I went to the boy's restroom, it is early in the morning noboby was in the park at all except for a city gardener and myself. What a mess the restroom is in, with graffitti all over the wall's, and clothes sprawled on to the cement floor. But it is my job to keep the restroom's clean. So I take a big black plastic bag from the plastic bag I had tied on to the big rolling plastic garbage can, and with my disposable working gloves on I pick up the clothes and throw them into the plastic bag. What a mess the restroom is in with wadded dried up toilet paper stuck to the ceiling's. Well the ceiling's are very high and the job of getting down the dried up toiltet paper will be left for the spring cleaning, I guess. The regular Janitor hadn't cleaned it for awhile look's like. Anyway I get tired of the supervisor's saving all the heavy cleaning for the on-call crew, yea they make us do the wall's and ceiling's and the scrubbing's, while the custodian's that are full-timer's and they get all the benefit's like their medical, dental, vacation pay, over time, sick leave and retirement, they have all of those benefit's and only do the job's of replenishing suppply's and the everyday stuff then us on-caller's get stuck with all the hard ass work, that's not fair. Anyway by the time those duty's come around again of doing the spring cleaning, I won't be working here anyway. I don't know really why I was even doing Janitorial work, I have a College Diploma. I guess I was about to find out why.

I finished cleaning the boy's restroom then I went over to the girl's restroom, and when I entered the bathroom, there on top of the sink was something that I had never ever saw in my life before. What the heck is it? I didn't know if maybe I should call animal control. I'm sure that all the other custodian's would have ran from it, but I was so used to dealing with animal's with my past work history, of working around animal's from large to small one's.

'Oh my gosh, it's, it's, it's, I don't know what it is.' It is shaped like a leaf, kind of oval, that is the best way to describe it's shape, although it's not a leaf. It's about eight inches wide, and twelve inches long. But what is it, I ask myself. It has zillion's and zillion's of 'thing's' on it that are all moving together in sequence. Never have I ever seen anything like it before, not on television or in a magazine. I was thinking that maybe it was a giant queen ant, you know how they swell up, but no it wasn't. It made like a weird sort of a soft toned humming sound, and as it moved there was a kind of a electrical spark to it. There wasn't any of them flying around, so me being such a dedicated worker to get the job done, I got a black plastic bag and hung it next to the sink then pushed the entire thing into the plastic bag with the sweeping broom end, tied the bag into a knot and finished cleaning the rest room. As I walked back to the main recreation building I dropped the black bag into a outside garbage can because I didn't want those 'thing's' inside of the building, or in my car that I drove to work with and had the broom in and supplies. Then I rolled the garbage can back to the building and put the small broom and the rest of the bag's into one large black bag, but didn't tie it closed, since I had to stop at another park before going back to the main recreation center where a full time custodian would be and where I would leave the small broom that I borrowed from there. I didn't like carrying around the big push broom that they had at the recreation center, so I just used the smalller broom to sweep up. It was almost lunch time by then so I stopped by the 'ol mansion to change my shoe's and take my lunch break. As I was driving in the small Datsun that I owned at the time I could feel what felt like something in my shoe's, and entering my body through the sole's of my feet. I immediately thought that it must be those 'thing's' entering my body, so when I got to the 'ol mansion I took off my shoe's and looked under them and into them and I saw nothing, but I could feel something like entering in through the sole's of my feet, but yet I didn't see any of those 'thing's' when I took off my sock's to check out the bottom of my feet. I changed my shoe's anyway and put on another pair of working boot's, then I went back outside to my Datsun and went to a drive through hamburger stand, bought me some lunch, parked in the parking lot and had my lunch.

After I ate lunch I went back to the main recreation center where I had gotten the supply's from that day to clean the other park in the hill's that had those 'thing's' at. When I got back to the main recreation center the full time custodian was there and she tell's me where is the small broom and not to use it anywhere out of that rec center and that it belong's there. Big deal it's just a darn small broom, So I pulled it out of the big black plastic bag and put back the other bag's that I didn't use.

"Hey what are those thing's on the broom?" She ask's me, but I hadn't noticed that there was some of those 'thing's' stuck to the broom, very tiny.

"Oh, I had to sweep up some 'thing's' that was in one of the restroom at Oak's park that Henry send's me to clean up twice a week."

"What are those thing's?"

"I don't know, they look like little half moon's and there was zillion's and zillion's of them on a large thing that was shaped like a large leaf but it wasn't a leaf, it was something hard that those 'thing's' were on, I don't know what they are, but I pushed them into a big plastic bag with that broom and threw the bag away into a garbage can outside the building there."

"But what are they, you should have called animal control."

"Yea, I know that now."

"Did any get on you? Damn I hope that they don't get on to me."

"I just hope they didn't get on me." I told her, but I didn't tell her what I felt like on the sole's of my feet."

"Well next time just use the broom there."

"The only broom's that they have there are those big push broom's, and I don't want to carry that big push broom to the outside restroom's, I can't sweep the restroom's right with those. Every time I leave the small broom's there, they get ripped off. I'll just see if I can get a small broom from Henry, and next time I won't leave the broom there but keep it in the back of my car."

"What are those thing's I never saw anything like them, do they jump?"

"I don't know what they do, or how they get around because I was sure not to touch them and kept a distance with the broom from them, except for sweeping that leaf thing with the broom into the plastic bag, but they managed to cling on to the broom anyway, damn they must have gotten in my car to because I had the open bag with the broom inside of it in my car too."

"Dang girl, you better clean out your cwar."

"Oh you mean my car, I heard that, I will."

Week's went by and I just didn't have the time to vacumn out my car. It had been awhile, since I had seen Jack, we just drifted apart. One of the custodian's asked me if I wanted to go and have a couple of beer's after work one day. His name is Randy, I found him attractive to me, as he is about the same age as I am, tall, dark and handsome, so I told him 'sure, I'll have a couple of beer's with you.' But then he doesn't have a car and take's the bus to work. See what I mean about the kind of men that I meet. So after work one day I waited for him at the corporation yard after work. We decided to buy a couple of six pack's and drive up to Redwood Road by the rifle range to a secluded spot where we really couldn't be seen from the road, but there is a nice view there, I pulled up my car there in that secluded spot, we sat in the car drinking the beer and smoking some green bud.

The weather, not too hot or cold, we sat there listening to some soul music and got higher and higher. Then Randy leaned over and kissed me, I kissed him back, our breathing got hot and heavy, one thing led to another so we climbed into the rear of my hatch back car where I had a blanket and a couple of designer pillow's. We layed next to each other on our side's making out. As we turned each other on, he take's a condom out of his wallet, I nod to him 'yes' and we had sex right there in the back of my car. Those hatch back's have enough space back there to roll around in a little. It was a quickie and we got our clothes back on just in time before a car passed by us as the people inside stared at us as we were just getting back into the front seat's. Randy got together all the empty beer can's and threw them out into the garbage can, and just as I started the car up to take off, here come's a Park Ranger, whew saved by the bell damn near. The Park Ranger watched us as we drove away, by that time I had come down and wasn't high anymore anyway.

I would see Randy all the time at work after that and he kept asking me to go and have some more beer's with him and if I would like to go out to dinner. But I alway's told him 'no,' because I just wasn't interested in him, he was good, but not that good. So we stayed on a friendly basis and said hi everytime we passed each other at work. He worked at the library's I worked at the park's. Until I got transfered to the police station and worked there.

But there was something happening in my car, I started to notice what looked like cigarette ashes by the stick shift, only it wasn't cigarette ashes that I found in my car, and even some on the back seat floor of the car. I compared whatever it is to cigarette ashes and they looked the same but it wasn't ashes. They were a little darker, kind of looked like some kind of animal dropping's. After all working in a Zoo for so many year's, I looked at crap all the time before raking or shoveling it up. I didn't know what those dropping's were or where they would come from. Then one day when I finially vacummed my car, I could swear that I heard like tiny shriek's sound's coming from under the car seat's when I vacumned up under there. Oh, so there was the condom under the blanket, I vacumned it up, and folded the blanket neatly.

'What the heck were those tiny shriek's as I vacumned?.' I thought to myself. Couldn't figure out that noise. I had also noticed that when I drove around town whenever I turned a corner I could hear something slide across the back of the car behind the back seat, I didn't have the seat's down, but there was a flat space behind the back seat. So I would pull over along side the road to check and see what that sliding noise was that was sliding across the back floor of the hatch back. When I looked and checked it, there was nothing there that could have been sliding across the back of the car and making that noise. So I drove and listened carefully and when I drove around a street corner and made a turn, I would hear that same sound again, like something sliding across the back of the car. There's that flat space back there because the car is a hatch back. Also many time's as I am driving in my car, I could heard a tiny sneeze, what in the world is the sneeze coming from, what was in the car with me?

'What the heck, what is in my car with me making those sliding noises when I turn corner's and where are those tiny sneezes coming from?' This all became a mystery to me even the ashy dropping's, 'what was in my car?'

Then to my surprise one day when I was watching television, I saw a scientist talking about some rock's that was found that had dropped to earth from Mar's. Then I couldn't believe what I saw next, there was a picture of these 'thing's' that were found on the rock's from Mar's, but the 'thing's' weren't alive anymore, but the scientist's believe that they once were. I looked at the 'thing's', and I knew what they were, they were some of those exact 'thing's' that I saw on that strange looking leaf shaped rock and cleaned them up at the restroom at Oak park, I called them 'skeezer's.' Now wait a minute this is all so unbelievable, those are the same 'thing's' and this scientist is saying that they came from Mar's, oh my GOSH. It's true those are the exact same thing's only the one's I saw and cleaned up weren't dead but alive. I had never seen those thing's anywhere except on television right now and that they are 'Martian's', on wow, oh WOW.

I went to the public library and looked through all the book's that I could find, I looked up every kind of bug, I couldn't find anything that even came close to those thing's. So according to the scientist's those are 'Martian's.' But what was I gonna do, catch some, but how. And that is what Dr. Raul told me to do when I went to the hospital to get a clearance to go back to work because those 'thing's' got all over me. They must of gotten all over the other custodian too, I was never scheduled to work in that area again, and I never went back to that bathroom, except one time year's later, saw nothing then, and that custodian so I have never seen her again till this day. Shortly after that happened with the 'thing's' I got transfered to work at the hall of justice.

But I had to go to the hospital to get medical attention for the 'thing's' on me. They were not just appearing on me but up under my skin, and I couldn't shake them off of me. One day I just felt like getting away for the night so I rented a motel room that has a nice hot tub for Eddie, a guy I was dating, and I to take a break away at and spend a couple of day's there. I went ahead of him to the motel that day and when I left for the morning as I usually do, I told him that I was going to work, but I ended up not going to work that day, I called in sick because of those 'thing's' me, at this point I hadn't went to see the doctor yet or I hadn't seen the t.v. program yet that has the picture's of the 'thing's' that the scientist's say they found in rock's from Mar's. Now remember the thing's the scientist's have in the rock's are very still and must be dead, I guess they look that way on film. But those exact 'thing's' I found on that leaf shaped rock are very much alive.

I told my stupervisor that I had a bad rash. He told me not to come back to work until I got a doctor's clearance to come back. I settled down into the motel room by myself and went over to the big grocery store at the shopping center next door. I went into there and bought some 'lice' remover hoping that it would work to get those thing's off of me. But by the time that I got back to the motel room and I opened the box it was empty. Someone had stolen the content's right out of the box, I had to go back to the store and get another one. I put the medicine on me, and I am not kidding when I got into the shower that day I thought of the 'thing's' might be from another planet because I had never seen anything like them, no where on this planet. At that time I hadn't seen the television program or the picture that came on the front of magazine cover's yet. And why did that all happen at the same time I discovered those 'thing's,' that really did turn out to be martian's straight from the planet of Mar's. There was just no other explanation for them, it was clear that they're the same thing's, a picture image of what is said to be from Mar's.

So I decided to go and see a medical doctor at the hospital he told me that he had never seen anything like this before. I told him I haven't either, but I never fully explained to him about the 'Martian's' I had cleaned up in the park restroom.

I knew right then that this doctor is a very intelligent person, and maybe he did really know but he wasn't saying anything about it, I don't know just maybe. I pointed out to him that there is a couple of different looking one's and told him that "Yes, I have seen picture's of them before." Only I didn't tell the good doctor where I seen the picture's at, but just evaded the question. Then he tell's me, "I tell you what, see if you can catch any of those 'things' and bring them to me."

I figured that he must have known because how in the heck was I actually gonna catch any of those 'alien's' since they were under my skin, literally, under my skin. He knew something, he had to have. But little did he know that I would actually take him up on that and someday bring him some of the 'captured Martian's.'

During those day's I lived in West Oakland, I lived with a kind family with my boyfriend back then. Dougie worked for the City of Oakland just like I did, but he had been laid off, and his brother Andrew still worked as a custodian where I did when I worked for the park's department. The two brother's, Andrew's wife Anabelle, his son, Lil' Jon, Dougie's mom, Dougie and I all had lived in the four bedroom apartment.

People would alway's stop to stare at us almost everywhere we went to together because I am light skinned, even though I am Hawaiian, Portuguese and Fillipino, born in Hawaii when King's and Queen's still ruled the island. So yes I will say in this year of 2015, I just made 65 year's of age. I try to stay out of the sun as bad as it is nowaday's to get into the sun, so my complexion stay's light. Well anyway, Dougie is black he is very dark, so that's why some people would turn their head's to look at us. I don't know what their problem is, so what, we were together, I really liked Dougie for awhile too, but he ended up being unfaithful at the end of our relationship, I'll tell you how I found out about it, one of his neighbor's got those 'thing's, the Skeezer's on her too and since it had been day's since I discovered the 'thing's from Mar's, I knew that Dougie must have had to get close to her for her to get that. No one else in the house had gotten them. So he had to have been with her. But I found all of this at the end of Dougie and my relationship and that is why I broke it off with him and left him, because of his messing around. I never did him wrong, even though I played alot if I found out that a man is messing around on me and doing me wrong then 'I drop him while it's hot,' and that's it between him and I!

Living in the apartment with his family got a little crowded sometime's, so as I usually do when I rent out a room is stay in my room most of the time, and Dougie would usually be right there with me. We had a great sex life together and would often walk to the park across the street, kitty corner to where we lived at. We would walk there together and stop at the store first to buy a couple of 30-ouncer's, then go and sit in the park, which was usually empty with no people there except us. We would sit on the swing's and swing back and forth while we conversate, sing and trip together on some weed and the beer, alway's keeping an eye for the passing police car's we poured our beer into our plastic cup's so it looked like we weren't drinking alcohol.

After the park that day, Dougie and I went back to the apartment and I just happened to look at the bottom of the shoe's that I wore the day I discovered the 'thing's', but this time I examined the shoe's extra close up. There were some on the bottom of the shoe's, but this time they weren't alive, but wedged in between the rubber part's of the bottom of my work shoe's. I got a toothpick and scraped them off and put them into a napkin, then I put them into a tight sealing avon container that I had, to keep them air tight. I told Eddie about Dr. Raul and how he asked me to bring him some of the 'thing's' if I could capture them. Hah, he thought that I would never be able to catch them but I did although I thought that I would never be able to catch them either. Now by this time I found out about what these 'thing's' are, they are Martian's, yes that is what they actually are, because the scientist's say they came from Mar's, that's what they said of the one's they have, they are the same exact looking 'thing's, just like the one's that came from Mar's embedded into a Mar's rock that I've seen photo's of, but the one's in the rock are either dead or dormant, the one's I found in that leaf shaped thing with the billion's and billion's of moving one's were very much alive and alive enough to get under people's skin. So many of them, with some swerving this way and other's swerving that way. Like I said I have never seen anything that even look's close to that anywhere all toghether like that, the only thing's that look like them are embedded into that rock the scientist's have that came from Mar's.

"Dougie, I'm gonna take this to Dr. Raul at the hospital, he told me if I could ever 'catch any' to take them to him." So we got into my car and drove to the hospital. I went to the front desk where I asked for Dr. Raul, they told me he is not in that day and wouldn't be back until next week. Well what was I gonna tell them to give the container with the 'Martian's' in it to Dr. Raul. No, I told Dougie to follow me to the swamp's. What! Swamp's in San Leandro, yes there are swamp's on the hospital ground's just above the parking lot area. As a matter of fact they had closed down that hospital year's later because it is sitting right on one of the earthquake vault line's. We went to the swampy area, I walked close to the murky water's and threw the container with the 'Martian's' in it, I threw it deep into the swamp. What else was I gonna do with it, I had to get rid of them. Did I mention the weirdest thing happened a few year's later that I saw when I had lived by that area again. I saw the City of some big company draining that swamp, I'm wonderering if that's what they were looking for. I just don't know I sure wasn't going to ask them, because I didn't know what they were draining that swamp for, heck they wouldn't admit it if that's what they were looking for, or just thought I was plain crazy.

As time went by and after Dougie and I broke up I had met another guy named Sammy. We had a relationship for awhile, but Sammy turned out to be a no good drunk. He lived with his mother, and was on disability and he take's alot of vallium and drink's with those too. I had to rent another room so I rented one from them. Sammy didn't seem all that bad when I met him to interview for the room for rent, and I knew from when I met him that we would end up going to bed together, and sure enought we did. But as time went by he proved to be a damn no good rotten thief and all around mess up. He ended up selling his mother's home in Oakland and buying a nice big three bedroom home in Stockton where he, his mother and I moved to. I didn't want to move out there but I did because I couldn't find another place to live with the budget that I kept at the time, so I moved out there with them about a hour away, when there was no traffic, but getting caught in traffic it would take much longer. It wasn 't to bad for me because I got transfered to a Recreation Center and didn't start work until 10:00 am, so I missed all the commute traffic.

Sammy's drinking along with the vallium's he was taking worstened, and he started treating his mother real bad, showing no respect for her, but then he had alway's treated her badly from day one. He even confided in me how he got over on insurance company's, claiming he got ripped off and collecting the insurance money when it was all bogus. He said he left his key's on top of his car and it got stolen, and that was in a high crime area of the city too. He must have known that it would be stolen. What a thief he is, I told him don't tell me anything else what you do, I just don't want to know. I couldn't take the way that he lived, drinking and real loud and real mean all the time, half out of his mind. I would be the one to drive his mom to the store and to her appointment's while I lived there. Then one day when he was drinking he told me to get out just like that, and he had the nerve to call the police on me when all I did around there was try to help them out, and pay him rent. I couldn't stand Sammy anymore, and regretted ever sleeping with him. The police said that he couldn't just throw me out like that and that he had to give me so many day's notice to move out. I told the police that I would be glad to leave if he would give me back my deposit and the full month's rent that I had given him in advance. Sammy got pissed off because I would no longer have sex with him, he turned out to be a real nut anyway. I mean getting pissy drunk, sometime's passing out on the couch and pissing in his pant's, treating his mother like crap, he was wrong to do that. I believe people should treat their parent's with the greatest of love and respect, and even any elder person, alway's have respect for your elder's is the way I was brought up. The only reason that he got the house was because of his mother that owned the house in Oakland and took that money to qualify for the big home, he didn't work.

He gave me back my deposit money for the room, and told me he would give me back the rest of the money next week if I came back there to get it. I got everything together, filled up my trunk, back seat and driver seat with boxes of my belonging's. I told him that I would pick up my Trek bicycle later, my work shoe's and a box of my favorite levi's next week when I come back for the rest of my rent money.

That damn biotch, I came back the following week for my expensive Trek bike and my other stuff and I brought Tony with me. He was my new guy I had met by then, I was now staying at his place in Oakland, it was closer to my job for the City of Oaktown anyway. I told Tony to stay there at the house in Oakland and wait for me while I went to get my belonging's from Sammy's house. But Tony took such a liking to me that he didn't want to let me out of his sight, unless it was when he went to work. I didn't mind that, I know some women don't like that but then Tony was smothering me with his feeling's, he was madly in love with me.

"Okay, you can come with me but wait in the car because if Sammy see's you he will get all jealous and he won't give me back my belonging's, especially my bicycle my Trek I for sure want that back."

"Okay, I will stay out of sight then, and wait in your car," Tony tell's me.

Tony doesn't own a car, he own's his own home in Oakland that his parent's willed to him, and he has a good job in security, but he doesn't own a car. So we drove to Sammy's place, and before I got out of the car I reminded Tony to sit in the car and don't show his face, because I knew how Sammy is. I go and knock on the front door and there is Sammy, he is about to let me into the house so I could get my belonging's, then Tony get's out of the car and show's his face. It was just like I said, now Sammy told me not to come into the house, and I told him I just want to get my Trek bicycle, work shoe's and levi's. He slammed the door and wouldn't let me get my stuff now. I asked Tony why didn't he stay in the car like I said. But I knew that he was very jealous of me and maybe thought that I was gonna do something else. But it wasn't like that, I was gonna do what I said that I was gonna do. I had to drive back there two more time's to try to get my belonging's, and finially called the police, but when the police got there they believed Sammy and not me. He told the cop's that he didn't have my stuff, but I knew what Sammy was up to. He had a dog door across the entrance of the front door and it was kind of high to walk over so when the officer lifted his foot to walk over the few feet high dog barrier, his foot knocked the dog barrier off whack and the officer apolgized to him for knocking it off whack and changed his mind about checking inside and just walked back to me telling me that I have to make a police report at the town's police station. And he also told me that someone had stolen my bike along with some of his computer's. The officer said "Yea, it was like he was trying to blame you for stealing all that stuff or something, well I don't believe him."

Yea, I thought to myself, then you don't actually believe me either, and if the officer did believe me then why didn't he go and check for my belonging's and my expensive Trek bicycle. I knew what Sammy was up to he must be making another fake claim on insurance again. Well I wasn't gonna be the one to tell on him, heck they probably woudn't look into the claim's anyway. After all I'm never believed everytime I make a complaint and tell the truth. Like those snake's I saw at the 'ol mansion, they never really checked into that, so why should I bother wasting my time. I gave up and quit trying to get my stuff back, Sammy is nothing but a drunken, hoe, disrespectful, lieing, lazy, good for nothing, useless thief. Someday it will all catch up to that biotch. I just let it go and called it a loss.

And that's what happened to those work boot's with some of the 'thing's, Skeezers" as I called them, on the bottom of them, Sammy has them along with my expensive Trek bicycle and my levi pant's. I even remember Sammy telling me that he could get twenty dollar's or more for used levi's at a clothes store in Berkeley. And that's why he stold them, what a low life thieving biotch he is! I had never seen him again after that, he got away with stealing some of my belonging's and the best bicycle I had ever owned. I bought the bicycle with some of the money my Mom gave me as a gift. Sammy's day will come if it hasn't allready.

If Tony wasn't such a jealous man, I know that I would have gotten back my belonging's that day. So now I had another boyfriend, and a very jealous one at that, why couldn't he just listen to some simple instruction's, heck that nice bike was never replaced. I went and bought me another good bike a Del Sol which is less than half the price that I paid for the nice Trek bicycle. Other people make mistake's and I end up having to pay for their mistake's, what a drag.

Now getting back to about the time after my co-worker and I had sex in the back of my Datsun car with the back seat down, after that time is when I would constantly hear tiny sneeze's while in my car. I would drive around by myself most of the time, and the car had it's radio pulled out of it, I only had the small portable radio, so mostly the battery's would be down and I drove around with no radio on, and no car heater either. I could hear clearly every noise around me. I kept finding the ashy dropping's all around inside my car, and hearing the tiny sneeze's, and the sliding noise coming from the back of the hatchback car each time I turned corner's in the car when I was driving, and even sometime's I feel like a small nip biting on my exposed ankle's.

Then one day when I washed my car and vacumned it out, reaching up under the seat's with the long nosed vacumn cleaner at the car wash, vacumning up the fast food that was left behind from when I ate in my car. Then while vacumning I could hear what sounded like little squeal's with the sucking up of the vacumn cleaner when I vacumned area's that couldn't be seen, like under the seat's and between them. 'What is that,' I just couldn't figure all this out.

And then it happened, after I drove away from the car wash, I was driving alone in my car, I had to know where all the sound's and sign's of something were coming from, like the sneezing, squealing, sliding and the ashy dropping's. So I just spoke out loud, and I just don't know what made me say this, but I said; "I know something is in my car, what is in here, who or what are you?" There was no answer.

"What or who is in this car with me, I know something is in my car with me, and whatever you are, I'm gonna set you free."

Then I heard them, but couldn't see them, whatever they are they said; "Fweeeeee, we're gonna be fweeeeeee!"

I almost couldn't believe what I was hearing, what in the world was it, or I should say what out of this world was it. It all flashed back to me about discovering those 'thing's' at the park restroom, on the sink top. But how did they get there, could it have been that the entire leaf shaped small montrosity form could also carry the leaf shaped figure and fly around. After all it had billion's and billion's of the tiny crescent shaped 'thing's' on top of it, those thing's that the scientist's call 'Martian's", because they say they are from Mar's that they found some inside of a rock, and some of those rock's had fallen to earth, and it was even the same time that I discovered those thing's that the scientist's said they fell to earth. Maybe that is how it got on top of the sink. Then I had put the broom that I had used to sweep them into the plastic bag, I had put it into my Datsun, and since some got on me, there must have been some of those 'Martian's' that got into my car. Of course, then I had sex in the car with Rick, and he had just thrown the condom that he used on the car floor, must of been some of those 'Martian's' got on to the condom and mixed with out bodily sex juices from the condom and evolved from that. That has got to be what happened, because shortly after that is when I started to find the ashy dropping's, and if they eat they must have eaten from the food that was left behind after I got food from drive through fast food place's and lived off of that, I guess that must be how they came about. There was just no other explanation to these 'thing's' that can now think and talk, they are actual alien's from Mar's and born here.

"Fweeeeee, we're gonna be fweeeeeee! You fwiend!" It sound's like there are a few of them, they sound so comical, and even laugh alot. Why was I not so shocked to know that these are actual Martian's. I guess mostly because they have been living amongst me, and actually right under my own nose. Living in my car for a long time now, month's at least. The sliding across the back of my hatchback car as I turned corner's, then checked to see what that noise was and there was nothing there on that back flat area that would slide, I had nothing back there at all, it was them, it was the tiny Martian's sliding across the back of my car when I made turn's.. The tiny sneeze's that I heard, and the food missing when I ate in my car at fast food's, the dark ashy dropping's, that was all from them. I could hear their little squeeky laugh's now, and it had been the first time that I actually tried to communicate with them, and come right out and say "I know that your there." They are so comical with their laugh's and squeeky talking. I've never been afraid of the Martian's, that I call Skeezer's, they just made theirselve's at home in my car. Yet I could sense that they can be real mean and harm a person or many people if they want to. But I know that if they are not messed with, then they keep away from people. Also remember I am a Animal Specialist, but these, I mean Wow.

"I know about you Martian's, and you can understand the word 'free'. You are mean little one's too aren't you! Please learn to be not so mean, and don't hurt anyone unless they hurt you. I am gonna take you to a nice spot in the hill's where you will have alot of area to live in, a place where there is alot of land to run around in and find food to eat and even water, there is a big pond there with fresh water and gold fish to eat, alot of fish." I know they like to eat fish by now because I would alway's buy deep fried fish and I finially figured out what happened to my fish when I used to eat it in the car, and turn my head away from my food, and then notice there would be a piece missing, but paid it not very much attention at the time. I had a small tray with short leg's on it that I would set on the passenger's seat, and put my food on the tray when I eat, and all the time when I ate, of course I wouldn't have my eye's on the food all the time, but turned my head as I eat, to look out the window at the scenery's, alot of time's I would park at the marina to watch the airplane's fly by above and watch the wave's curl into the shore or watch the bird's. But too many time's when I would be sitting in my car and eating and go for another piece of fish to eat, the fish would look like some pieces was broken off. I could never figure that out, all the time it would happen, but now I know it was the Martian's, I know that they move real fast, as I will tell you that I caught a glimpse of some of them, and they move very fast, very, very fast.

This is all so unbelievable but the proof is all there, and it is true, this really happened! I drove up to the Oakland hill's to a spot that I had been going to for year's and year's to have picnic's, usually with whatever boyfriend I have at the time, and many time's by myself. Picnic's, listening to music, smoking weed and drinking beer is just something I enjoy doing. Or many time's I have been up there alone, and have been going to that same spot for many year's, since I was a teenager. But I hadn't been up there for awhile, as a matter of fact from before I had sex in the car with Rick.

I drove to the hilly spot, it is so nice there, with tall green eucalyptus tree's swaying and making creaking sound's with the breeze of the wind swaying the tree's back and forth. Alot of grassy area's, and a nice big pond that flow's down the hillside, and even has alot of Koi fish in it. I know this would be a nice spot for the 'Martian's.' But first, of course, I had stopped at the store and bought two can's of beer. I would drink only a beer or two because I had to drive.

I'm thinking that I never leave my car door's open for too long, just to get in and out of the car. I never bought alot of groceries since I am a single woman and just eat out at different place's all the time, or in a restaurant here and there. Because if I had loaded alot of groceries into my car then I would have left the door open for a while, but I never did.

I pulled up to the nice spot over looking across the bay and on to San Francisco, and parked there on to a dirt area real close to picnic table's and bar-b-q pit's. I knew instinctively that the Martian's would have to have a way of escape, and that even though they are fast, there must be a reason that they hadn't left my car yet, but had continued to live in the car. So I grabbed me one of those cold one's from the brown bag in the passenger's seat, got my transistor radio, put my key's in my pant's pocket. I left all the window's in the car all the way down so the Martian's could get out of there, then I walked over to a picnic table and sat there looking out to the beautiful view of the city's down below and over to San Francisco. I didn't trun around to look at my car because I just knew that the Martian's wouldn't want me to see them getting out of the car. I gulped down one beer it tasted so good. I went back to my car to get the other cold beer.

I walk over to my car and am about to open the driver's side door and looking through the rolled down window of the driver's side and unbelievably to my eye's, there sitting between the two front bucket seat's was one of the Martian's. We looked right into each other's eye's, and in a split second she was gone. She is very fast, but for that split second I saw her, I knew it was a female, she looked very pregnant with a big belly. She has dark skin, she looked about nine inches long, and has arm's and hand's, but I couldn't see the lower part of her because from well below her waist to the bottom part of her, that part of her was hidden behind the driver's bucket seat. She has black hair that is straight and curls up at the end's like a poof hairstyle, and she has my face feature's. Although I hadn't noticed a nose on her, and if she had one it was very small. Her mouth isn't too big, but her eye's are unforgettable. For that split second when I saw her, I know it is true, she is a Martian, well part Martian, and must have been concieved from that condom left from Rick and I, I feel very attached to the Martian's.

I knew why she sat there, she was pregnant and couldn't get out of the car through the rolled down window's. I sat in the driver's side for a minute, shaking my head in disbelief. I couldn't believe what I just saw, but I know I saw it, a real life Martian that was born from those 'thing's'. Because the "Skeezers" had been left on that broom which had been set in my car. Somehow they must have mingled with that condom.

I got the brown bag with the last beer in it, I was gonna need to drink down that beer real fast now, after seeing what I just did. I got out of my car and left the driver's side door open half way and walked over to the other side of the car and opened that door halfway also and left it open. But just as I started to walk over to the picnic table a car pull's up, a small white older car with a older man in it maybe in his sixty's. He pull's up to the side of the road and park's. He is staring at me, I tell him, 'what you looking at?' He tell's me 'why do you have to be so mean?' Then I just walk away to a picnic table, he pull's away and drive's further down the hill. I walk back over to my car to look down the road both way's and make sure the man is gone then just as I am turning around I notice one of those Martian's carrying a baby Martian in it's mouth and just scrambling into a bush and toward's the monument that is in the picnic area. I just couldn't tell how they ran, their body position was running, yet it was kind of sliding, like the lower part was half snake. The female pregnant Martian was sitting up like a tiny person, allthough I didn't see her from the waist down because she was sitting between the bucket seat's of the driver and the passenger side's. Oh gee, I saw another one, this is all unbelievable, except that I know it is true because of all of the sign's that the Martian's left behind, like their dropping's and the other sign's. I went back over to the picnic table and snapped open that beer, gulped that down, threw the can into the garbage can near by. Then as I am sitting there I can hear the most beautiful sound of something singing, what I could compare it to is like a wonderful bird singing, but it wasn't bird's singing, I knew that it was the Martian's, they were happy. I had never since then, before then or ever in my life heard that beautiful singing sound again, it sounded so beautiful. If I only had a camcorder or a cell phone at that time, I could have captured the sound, but that was in the early 1990's and all I had then was a pager. The Martian's are so fast that I probably could not have gotten them on film but at least I could have captured that sound, the beautiful song. It was so beautiful a song, I knew that the Martian's are very happy to be free, like they said "Fweeeeeeee." I had been to that spot in the hill's hundred's of time's before and I had never ever heard anything like that before, this was all new to me, all of it, they really are Martian's.

After all what could I do, I would never be able to capture one of them, not now not the way they are, real being's. I just wanted them to be free in this world and not to be dissected or experienced on. I really didn't know how many of them were there. I drove down the hill to a small store and bought another beer. Then yet something else happened as I was driving down to the store I could smell a strange smell I don't know what it is, and like all the other sign's that the Martian's left behind I had never smelled that kind of a odor in the air, but the odor was coming from my car. Then I realized that it must be a smell from the Martian's, and the nest of a home they had made somewhere in my car. Now their little home was empty, but at least they are somewhere safe, as long as nobody knew of them and where they are, they will be okay, I hope. I kept this to myself, after all I couldn't go around telling people this, who would believe me anyway, but it is true and not a figment of my imagination. All of the physical evidence that they left behind, and when they spoke to me and what I saw, I saw them, it is all true, it really happened. I heard the noises they make, so many time's, the sneezing, the sliding in the back of the car, and now they are free to live in the outdoor's. I made sure to leave them by a statue there where they could live and hide inside of where nobody can bother them, those statue's have been there for as long as I remember, even when I had first went there when I was a teenager, year's before, and there are small opening's that lead into and under the statue, they will be safe there.

My lifestyle changed after that, and I no longer drove up to those hill's to kick it up there and look at the beautiful scenery or sit amoung the tall tree's in the picnic area. Although I went back there a few time's within a couple of month's later, I still never saw them again. The sound's of the tiny sneezes in my car, and the sliding coming from the back of the car and the dropping's, and food missing all stopped, that never happened in my car anymore. I gave the car to my son, and it still ran like a top, and all that time I never had a problem with it, I sure got my money's worth for more than the ten year old car. My son sold it later. Wow, I sure would like to have that old Datsun today.

I went to visit that same spot where I let the Martian's free some year's later, everything looked so different. The area was no longer green, the tree's looked to be stripped of their beauty, and the area looked so different, and didn't have all the nice life it had before. After going there for all those year's why had that area changed now. Was it the Martian's that did that to the area of the park that I set them free at, that I just don't know for sure. I no longer couldn't get to exact area where I let the Martian's run free at because now thing's have changed and that area is gated off. I could have walked to get to that area, and maybe sometime in the future I will. However I can tell you that they are still there, I just know it, that rock they came from originated in Mar's. All that happened around 1995. After I let the Martian's go that day yes, I never heard them in my car again, nothing ever again. They are real, so very real.

BEAUTIFUL CROSS VISION

My mother, Ida, God rest her soul, was a wonderful woman, mother, wife, grandma, auntie, sister, and friend to people. In 2002 I found out she had cancer of the lung's, even though she never smoked. But she had worked for Gerber's Baby Food's in Oakland, California back in the 1950's, 60's, and early 70's, retiring in 1974. Mother would wear a button on her white work smock, I was a small girl at that time, and I asked her what that button on her smock was for, she told me she had to wear it because in the section that she worked at the baby food bottle's would have to go through a x-ray machine, so that meant radiation, then she said that she had to keep an eye on her button because when it would turn red that would mean she would have to leave that section because the radiation got to high, but she wasn't the only worker with those button's on, there were other's too. Okay so I'm thinking maybe that's how she got the lung cancer from working at Gerber's Baby Food's. Year's later they had closed down and moved to another state, probably to avoid lawsuit's.

I cared for mom in her last month's of life, you couldn't really tell she was sick, she still had energy and looked beautiful for her age of 77, and did everything on her own, including gardening, she loved her beautiful flower's, and her yard was so pretty it could be on the cover of a magazine. Mom told me about a month before she passed away that if she had a cross it would be a plain cross. About three week's before mom passed a surgeon at the hospital that she had been going to for her appointment's said she would need surgery, and that he would start on one lung on one side first. I asked mom what she wanted to do, and that it was up to her, she said she might as well have the surgery, because she did have alot of pain sometime's, but she was such a strong woman, and hated to complain, and didn't want to take any pain medication either. The surgeon, which was also her doctor a Dr. Was, said mom would have her surgery and we could bring her home in a few day's later. Before the surgery when they called out my mom's name, "Ida", to go in for the surgery, we were with her, and I felt a moving butterfly sensation within myself, like a butterfly moving within me, a feeling I had never had before. If only I knew then what that feeling meant, it meant that my mother was not going to survive that surgery. I would have told Mom, "Don't go Mom, don't go", but I didn't know and I thought the surgeon would know what he would be doing to help mom. Another strange thing happened that Mom had told me about. About a couple week's before her surgery she got a phone call from a lady whom she did not know who it was, but the lady told her "Don't go, don't go, don't go outside, don't go". What that lady meant, Mom did not know. Make's me wonder if that lady that called Mom that day, whom Mom said sounded like she had a oriental accent when she spoke, well maybe she knew something about the surgery, and was trying to warn Mom, we just didn't know.

After the surgery Dr. Was came out to the lobby just when Pop, my dad, mom's husband had just gotten up to use the restroom, what timing I thought. So Dr. Was sat down and drew a diagram of the surgery he performed on mom, and that he wedged out part's of mom's left lung, but that she would be allright, and told me we could take her home on Thursday, We saw mom after the surgery, she didn't look too good. then again hour's later, when we went to visit her that Wednesday evening she told me she never wanted to have that kind of surgery again. Dr. Was, he was there too kind of hanging around it seemed like. He told me that he wanted to move mom out of the ICU and into a private room. Till this day I regret what Dr. Was did, he shouldn't have moved mom out of the ICU, he told me the other room would be more quiet for my mom. But when they rolled mom to the other room, she told me right away that she did not like it in that room. There was another patient in that room and she had the TV on real loud, also there was no clock in that room. Oh gosh, I miss mom so much and it hurt's alot to write about what happened to mom. Later that evening, before me and Pop left my mother asked me for a kiss goodbye. I reached over and barely reaching her I kissed her, not knowing that would be the last kiss goodbye, while she was alive. Early the next morning mom called me and complained that she was so hungry, I guess she would be since they took her off of the IV she was getting. I spoke with her nurse that told me she would be eating soon. Me and Pop were going to visit Mom, but then I got a phone call from Dr. Was, he say's "Your Mom she's not doing well, and she's not going to make it". I told him we would be right there, I drove to the hospital speeding, pulled up in front, not caring if my car got towed, I just wanted to hurry for my mom. When we got to Mom's room, she was lying there, she had passed away. Part of my world ended right then and there, I was the closest to Mom then any of the other kid's. Both Pop and I cried, I called two of my kid's that came straight to the hospital, she was very close to them too. Mom made Pop and I promise when she was sick that we told no one, and we told no one. My son, Mom's Grandson stayed with Mom until the mortuary in San Leandro took Mom away, even after the funeral, my son, Mom's Grandson, sat there at the graveyard, next to his Grandmother's coffin, waiting for them to bury her. A grave digger told Paul that he could not stay there anymore. He told them that he wasn't going anywhere until they finish burying his Grandmother. And he stayed there until she was completely covered. Oh Mom, I love you so. I cried for 24 hour's straight, Mom's gone. As soon as I got home that day, because my boyfriend, whom is now my husband we lived with my parent's in my parent's home, but as soon as I got home that day, I heard Mom's voice say "It's wonderful here". Absent from the body, present with the Lord. Mom was a wonderful person, I loved her so very much. I promised her I would take care of Pop, and now he live's with me and my husband in Oakland, he is 94 year's of age. At Mom's Rosary, when she was on view, I gave her one last kiss, she was my mother, "Honor Thy Father and Thy Mother".

Something strange though, the funeral parlor told me Mom had a big cut from the surgery on her lower back side, I can't be sure if it was the right side or left side, but I think they said on the left side. I don't know what the surgeon would be doing cutting Mom on that area of her body, make's me wonder. I just don't know, but I still wonder about that until this day. I called the hospital day's later and told them I was coming in there and that I wanted to read my mother's medical paper's when she was in the hospital. My sister-in-law came with me, we looked through Mom's medical paper's, and we found it kind of strange that the surgeon Dr. Was he was sort of hanging around in the next room to see what we were doing, I could see him through an opened door, he never came over to talk with us either.

Now, about the beautiful cross. The day marked seven year's that Mom had passed on. I was sitting in my front room, by myself after dinner watching TV, when something on the wall caught my eye. I looked at it and I couldn't believe what I was seeing, I then looked around to see where this vision was coming from. Then I knew it was not of this world, it appeared to me, it was a cross on the wall, it was a 'plain cross' like Mom said she would want. Only this cross was so beautiful, it was shining, shimmering and putting off fantastic spark's, it had a light coming from it like no other shiny light I had ever seen before. It was a beautiful cross, shining, shimmering, putting out spark's of light. I wanted to go get my camera to take a picture of it, or go get Pop to see it, but then I also did not want to leave, I wanted to keep watching it, every moment of this wonderful cross I could see. It lasted for a short while then started to dissappear from the ouside toward's the center in a circle motion, then it was gone. After it dissappeared, I shook my head with disbelief, but I know what I had just seen. Was that cross a sign from Mom, it did mark seven year's she was gone. All I know is that it was so beautiful and it was real and not of this world, I knew it was a Holy cross.

I have seen a few thing's in my life, thing's that most people will never ever get a chance to witness. This world is not just grey and white, it has many color's, I know what I have seen in my lifetime.

LITTLE GREEN MEN AND THE DEVIL

In 1983 when I was with my boyfriend at the time, we were together from 1982 until 1988. His name was Fred, he was living in a small house behind his sister's home on 103rd avenue in

Oakland, California. I would go to spend the night with him quite often, in those day's that was right after I sold my home in Hayward and I bought a Toyota, Dolphin motorhome, I also lived in it. It was actually a blast parking at a friend's home or my brother's driveway at night and then park at the San Leandro Marina during the day when after I woke up I would drive to the Marina, shower, cook me some breakfast, and start my day's of partying all over again. I was collecting unemployment benefit's for about a year and living off the money of the sale of my home. I just couldn't find a good job for awhile as later I went to work for the United States Post Office. Okay so one evening I went to see Fred, we were kicking back in his bed, talking in the dark, then I noticed some tiny light's coming from his ceiling and I asked Fred if he had sparkles on his ceiling, he said "No, he didn't." then he turned on the light and we looked up at the ceiling, sure enough there were no sparkles on his ceiling, he then turned the light back off, the sparkles came back. We laid there still talking then I noticed a white spear looking object in the upper corner of the room, a ladder came down from it and little green men were climbing up the ladder. Then there appeared a green glowing orb that was dashing around the room, and then there started to appear, well it looked like the devil himself, he had two spiral pointed horn's, evil wicked eye's, and a evil smile on his face. Fred was so scarde that he saw it and hid under the blanket. I began to pray, "I plead the blood of Jesus Christ, satan flee". And at that moment that devil took the form of the green orb again and flew right through the wall, to outside. Fred, and I just sat there in the bed in disbelief, we didn't talk much more that night. That morning he went to work I went to visit my mother. I pulled up alongside my mother's home, she came to the door and looked at me and said to me, "You better come inside here, it look's like you saw the devil", I said "Oh my goodness, Mom, I did see the devil". So my mother knew what I saw and I had not spoken to her before she saw me that day. My mother alway's just knew certain thing's, and she believe's in God, and she had been reborn as a Christian, and love's the Lord, dearly, she raised me the same way. When Mom looked at me and told me it look's like I saw the devil, it really verified that Fred and I had really saw the devil. That was the only time in my life my mom ever said that to me.

A day had passed by, I went to visit Fred again, I asked Fred "Please draw me a picture of what you saw that night". He drew an exact picture of what I saw also, all the little detail's that one would only know unless they saw it themself. Night's after that I took my 35 mm camera and tried to get a photo, we never saw it again. Actually I'm glad for that it was quite frightening.

THE GIANT FISH IN THE SKY

I can't forget this day, in the morning my dad and I went to visit my Cousin, she had breast cancer, it was the last time we saw her alive, month's later she passed away, rest her soul. After I came back home, I got my pet dog "LuLu", and I took her with me to the Bay Fair Mall to the pet store there, my dog's needed dog food, bone's and a new outfit for LuLu. I also had to take back a fish that I had bought from the petstore the day before it had died in the fish tank, so I took the fish to show to the clerk in the fish department. I don't think I bought another fish, it was bad enough what happened to that one. Upon coming out of the pet store I set the dead fish that was in a plastic bag on the curb by my car, then something told me, well you know that little voice inside that sometime's tell's you to do or to say something, well something told me to 'get my camera out and take a picture', then I thought why would I want to take a picture. I proceeded to put LuLu in her car seat in my Smart car. When I came around to the other side of my Smart car to get in, I looked up and I saw in the sky a huge, giant fish in the sky. Wait, now this was not a blimp, it was too close and too big to be a blimp, yes it was bigger than a blimp, and it sure was not a kite. There was a woman just standing there, she was in black, I told her, "What is that thing in the sky?" She just shrugged it off, and said "Oh, Idunno", and she say's "Oh, I like your Smart car," and started asking me alot of question's about my Smart car. I looked up at the sky at this, this thing, gigantic, huge. The thing about it was it looked like a fish, but it's eye's they were moving around and the eye's looked real. There were window's on the side of it, I kept trying to see if I would see any people or perhap's 'alien's' in those window's. I was gonna get my cell phone or camera, by now the year was about 2010, I just happened to have my camera with me that day because I was gonna take picture's with my cousin, but never did. But that woman kept talking to me, acting like it was no big deal about the fish in the sky. Thinking back, you know how they say there are 'men in black', I believe she was a 'woman in black'. Because of her, I never took a picture, which was really rare for me because I love taking picture's, I have thousand's of photo's on hard copy, CD's and on my computer. Then when I looked up again, I asked her' "Hey, what happened to that huge fish in the sky, she shrug's it off again and say's "Oh, I dunno, it must have floated off that way." I'm thinking back, that was a UFO, it made no noise, just hanging there in the sky, in broad daylight, and it was much bigger than a blimp. In my career also while working at a Zoo, I bacame a Animal Specialist, I know about animal's, I know that UFO was alive, and it's eye's were real. Darn, I missed taking a photo because of that 'woman in black'. I don't think I will ever get a chance to see anything like that again. I checked on You Tube and saw some video's of fishes in the sky, but nothing like the one, me and that 'woman in black' saw.

DRIVING AROUND, DAY OF WEIRDNESS

Just adding to my story here some strange thing's that I have experienced and saw. I remember it was a holiday, Memorial Day. During those day's I drove around alot, and I mean alot, I would stay within the cities of San Leandro, Hayward, and Oakland, California where I live. But in those day's I was single, my kid's grown, I was on my own and while working for the City of Oakland I rented room's, having to keep moving alot because the places I lived would alway's end up being renting from some kind of weird people, all the time, it was terrible. I would rent a room, pay the owner or manager first, last and deposit to stay there, then after I move in, and I mean move in. I used to get a moving company to move some of my thing's from storage like, my bedroom set and some boxes. I just don't know why I had never stop to think why didn't I just move with a suitcase, it would have been much easier on me. But I just wanted to make a home for myself. But every place, and I mean every single place turned out to be messed up. People whom would live in the same house renting a room or two for themselves would enter my room when I would be gone or at work and steal from me or worst. So I would drive around alot just to not be there, or looking for another place to live. It just never worked out, I would stay somewhere and people would bother me, then when I move the people I rented from would keep my deposit or last month's rent. All rip offs, I had never found a honest person out of them all. So I'm driving around then first on the freeway I see a big bloodied dog body on 880 freeway in San Leandro, someone must have driven over it, I don't know what it was but it looked scary seeing it on the freeway. Then the same day I was driving down Marina boulevard in San Leandro and laying on the middle divider was a stiff black cat, I mean a stiff cat laying on it's back and leg's in the air, what was that about. I was drivng down 73rd avenue in Oakland coming around the bend at the top of the hill, as I turned the bend I looked in my rear view mirror and what looked like two black snake's standing erect fighting each other, how weird. Now that was a strange day of what I saw while driving, never had a day like that again.

THE TINY FAIRY

I had a favorite tree in Hayward on Industrial Blvd. The tree is very tall, a eucalyptus tree, I would ride my bike there to have a few beer's in the evening sometime's. Heck, I went there so much that I had a dream one night that the tree was crying. But what I saw one night was not a dream, I was sitting on some grass next to the tree, sipping on beer, I was not drunk I had only a couple of beer's that night. For a moment when I was looking into the tree at the branches and leave's as the wind blew them gently I saw a tiny Fairy appear, and she was gone. She was bright, had a tiny wand and little wing's, and actually did look like the many picture's people draw of tiny Fairy's. Also, think of the many, so many people that witness to seeing actual Fairy's, doesn' that count for something? Well, I am telling you I am one of those people that witnessed it. I was not expecting to see that tiny Fairy and I have never saw another one.

LOVING PET DOG'S

I had a beautiful black and white Pomeranian dog named LiLi, on her chest was a white star, her paw's white, except one paw was black. She was such a loving dog. One day there was a Poodle dog that attacked her, I was on my way to take LiLi to the veterninarian but she died. It was so very sad. That evening when I went to sleep, I turned off all the light's as usual. Then upon falling asleep I could see a standing shaped oval beautiful crystal like image, it appeared to be some kind of an opening to another world. It was so pretty, then I opened my eye's and it was no longer there, then I closed my eye's and it was there again, I just kept looking at it, then at the bottom of it I noticed something black and white jumping, rolling and hopping so happily, I kept looking at it and I could see that it was "LiLi'. Although she had died earlier that day, she was there so happy. I still couldn't believe what Iwas seeing so I closed my eye's again, and there was that beautiful standing oval shaped crystal opening and there was LiLi, so happy, she then jumped right into the crystal opening. I kept watching the crystal opening and it floated there then moved off and away real fast toward's the right. How amazing I thought, it was there when I closed my eye's, but gone when I opened my eye's.

A couple of year's later my loving Chihuahua, Scooby Doo died, he died from old age, almost 100 year's old, in dog's life year's, they are 7 year's to one person's year's. It was real sad too, one night he started breathing heavy, by the time I went upstair's and came back down, Scooby looked at me, and he took his last breath and died. Scooby would go so many places with us, store's, visiting people, the beach, like LiLi. I miss them both so very much. That night I went to bed, turned off all the light's and the crystal door opening appeared again. But this time I was sort of expecting it, because of what happened when LiLi died. I saw the crystal opeing, then I saw Scooby jump right into it. And it was the same I saw the crystal opening when my eye's were closed. I love all animal's, I miss those two dog's a whole lot.

STORY ENDING

It has taken me 25 year's now to write this book. Once this is published I will start working on another. What I have written about in this book is true, but of course it's up to the reader to believe it or not. But if you really knew me, you would know that I do not make a practice of lie's, believe me it's true.

But what is not true is Jack and I being so close, there is a Jack, but that is not his real name, and we never had a relationship like all the time's I wrote of being together in this book. It was a one time thing, but I still feel for Jack. He want's nothing to do with me. I am the kind of person that only need's to be told once, I simply walked away from Jack after he told me that I never bothered him again. If he don't want me, well then I don't want him.

martiansofoakland@gmail.com

About the Author

I was born in Hawaii and our family came to Oakland, California when I was three. My Dad is a WWII Pearl Harbor survivor, U. S. Navy. My Mom worked at Gerber's Baby Food's for year's. Both are loving, caring and kind parent's. I grew up in Oakland but throughout my life I moved around quite a bit. From Oakland to San Leandro, Hayward, Union City, Berkeley, San Francisco and back to Oakland. I have tried my best to do what's right throughout my life, and treat people and animal's kind. I love family, pet's, writing, music, art, car's, excercise and cooking.

Printed in the United States
By Bookmasters